...gibbered and fell back for a moment,

a terrible twittering noise, like that of thousands of bats, filling the air and echoing on and on through the complex of chambers.

Bac Puri's sword swung to left and right, up and down, slicing off limbs, stabbing vitals, piercing the unnaturally soft, clammy bodies.

And then he was, as if by magic, a mass of spears. He howled in his pain and madness as javelins like the one we had seen earlier appeared in every part of his body until it was almost impossible to distinguish the man beneath.

He fell with a crash.

Seeing the creatures were at least mortal, I decided we should take advantage of Bac Puri's mad attack and, waving my sword, I leapt through the entrance, shouting:

"Come—they can be slain!"

They could be slain, but they were elusive creatures and sight and feel of them brought physical revulsion. With the others behind me, I carried the attack to them and soon found myself in a tangle of soft, yielding flesh that seemed boneless.

And the faces! They were vile parodies of human faces and again resembled nothing quite so much as the ugly little vampire bat of Earth. Flat faces with huge nostrils let into the head, gashes of mouths full of sharp little fangs, half-blind eyes, dark and wicked— and insensate.

As I fought their claws, their sharp teeth and their spears, they slithered about, gibbering and twittering.

I had been wrong about them. There was not a trace of intelligence in their faces—just a demoniac blood-hunger, a dark malevolence that hated, hated, hated— but never reasoned.

My companions and I stood shoulder to shoulder, back to back, as the things tore at us...

Praise for Michael Moorcock

"The greatest writer of post-Tolkien British fantasy."
—*Michael Chabon, author of*
The Amazing Adventures of Kavalier & Clay

"Vastly entertaining."
—*William Gibson, author of Neuromancer*

"A writer of undeniable talent."
—*Lin Carter*

"Michael Moorcock is a true literary wonder.
I'm a lifelong reader and fan."
—*Greg Bear, author of Darwin's Radio*

"Unquestionably the most varied and prolific of SF authors."
—*A Reader's Guide to Science Fiction*

"The most important UK fantasy author of the 1960s and 1970s,
and altogether the most significant UK author of sword and
sorcery, a form he has both borrowed from and transformed."
—*The Encyclopedia of Fantasy*

"If you are at all interested in fantastic fiction,
you must read Michael Moorcock"
—*Tad Williams, author of Shadowplay*

THE PLANET STORIES LIBRARY

The Ginger Star by Leigh Brackett
The Secret of Sinharat by Leigh Brackett
The Anubis Murders by Gary Gygax
The Samarkand Solution by Gary Gygax
Elak of Atlantis by Henry Kuttner
City of the Beast by Michael Moorcock
Lord of the Spiders by Michael Moorcock
Black God's Kiss by C. L. Moore
Northwest of Earth by C. L. Moore

STRANGE ADVENTURES ON OTHER WORLDS

AVAILABLE MONTHLY EXCLUSIVELY FROM PLANET STORIES!

FOR AUTHOR BIOS AND SYNOPSES,
VISIT PAIZO.COM/PLANETSTORIES

Planet Stories is a division of Paizo Publishing, LLC
2700 Richards Road, Suite 201
Bellevue, WA 98005

PLANET STORIES is a trademark of Paizo Publishing, LLC

Visit us online at paizo.com/planetstories

Printed in China

Planet Stories #8, *Lord of the Spiders*, by Michael Moorcock
First Printing March, 2008

10 9 8 7 6 5 4 3 2 1   2007

Lord of the Spiders

— OR —

Blades of Mars

by Michael Moorcock

Originally published as by Edward P. Bradbury
Introduction by Roy Thomas
Cover by Andrew Hou

PLANET STORIES
Seattle
Erik Mona, Publisher

Michael Moorcock and the Spiders of Mars

INTRODUCTION BY ROY THOMAS

RICHARD A. LUPOFF said it all about pastiches, I think—as well as anybody else ever did or could—in his 1965 study *Edgar Rice Burroughs: Master of Adventure*:

"To the extent that a successor author maintained fidelity to the original, his work was superfluous. To the extent that it varied from the original, it tended to fracture the structure of imagination created by the original author."

In other words, writing a pastiche of (or, to use another common phrase, an "homage" to) an established work or genre of literature is a double-edged sword. Stick too close to the pattern, and why bother doing it at all? Deviate too greatly, and you're probably going to vitiate the effect you were striving for, maybe even to the point where people may not recognize what you're pastiching.

So then, why write a novel in the style and set in the general milieu of another author?

Well, there's always the money.

Now don't wrinkle up your nose that way. After all, there's something—not everything, but *something*—in Dr. Johnson's old adage that, "No man but a blockhead ever wrote, except for money." Bills must be paid, by young authors and old ones, and there are far less pleasant ways to earn a paycheck than to scribe a pastiche.

Still, there *are* other reasons—valid reasons, I think—for writing stories in close imitation of another's style and subject. The late Lin Carter, himself a pastichist, once put it this way: "One writes the books that one wants to read."

So if Edgar Rice Burroughs only wrote roughly a dozen novels in his groundbreaking and immensely popular Martian series—and if you have read them all, and want to read more—and if nobody else is doing it quite the way you think it should be done—why, then, you take a stab at writing it yourself!

Back in the 1960s, when the Burroughs boom was in full bloom, it seemed as if every week saw the paperback racks visited by a new "homage" to the creator of Tarzan, John Carter of Mars, Carson of Venus, David Innes of Pellucidar, and all the rest. And the interplanetary-slanted "pocket books" were generally the pick of the litter.

And Michael Moorcock was one of the best of the pastichists.

Why are we not surprised?

For, most of the "homage-enizers" were either writers best remembered for other things (the aforementioned Lin Carter for his anthologies that introduced readers to fantasy writers unjustly relegated to dusty bookshelves—Gardner Fox for the comic books for whom he created the Flash, two Hawkmen, the Justice Society, and so many others—Robert E. Howard, author of the John Carterish *Almuric*, for sword-and-sorcery heroes Conan and King Kull)—

—or else they were writers soon forgotten, along with their derivatively named books.

Michael Moorcock, however, was (and is) that *rara avis*, the man who could pen a nigh-perfect pastiche, catching the nuances of ERB as well as Otis Adelbert Kline or anyone else ever did—*and* one who could turn a pastiche into something far more than mere imitation, a house of art in its own right.

The primary example of the latter, of course, is Moorcock's creation Elric of Melniboné, whose roots are twined about the fiction of Bob Howard and yet who is also a separate literary entity all his own—a vertitable *anti-Conan*, in fact.

And a good example of Moorcock's prowess at the pastiche, pretty much pure and simple, is the youthful trilogy that the current editors call the "Kane of Old Mars" series, of which *Lord of the Spiders* is the middle part. This is the paperback original that, back in 1965, was christened *Blades of Mars* when its British author was impishly suggesting by his byline that he might be a kinsman of another Bradbury who liked Burroughs.

To enter the world of Michael Kane is basically to discover three more Martian novels by ERB, with the names changed to protect, well, not so much the innocent as the well-intentioned. And those names are mostly good ones, suggesting their Barsoomian lineage without veering too close to literary pickpocketing: Vashu—Bac Puri—Jewar Baru—Shizala—Hool Haji.

Yes, most of all—Hool Haji.

You've gotta love an author who can coin a name like that with a straight face.

Or *did* Michael Moorcock have a straight face when he banged out *Warrior of Mars* and its two fast-moving sequels at what just *has* to have been a manual typewriter?

Maybe, instead, he was laughing his ass off the whole time as he banged away at the keys—having a great time, not because he was trying to fool anybody, not really, into thinking he was Edgar Rice Burroughs, but because he wanted to give a few hours' entertainment to folks who had read everything from *A Princess of Mars* to, Issus help us, *The Skeleton Men of Jupiter* and who didn't want to imagine their world without still more Burroughsian fantasies to read. Probably, neither did Moorcock.

The man delivered, both as Michael Moorcock *and* as Edward P. Bradbury.

And I'll bet he had fun being both authors!

Just as I had fun reading the books in the 1960s, and have enjoyed dipping once again into Martian canals of the mind that will never run dry.

Roy Thomas
December, 2007

ROY THOMAS *is the former Editor-in-Chief of Marvel Comics, and has written stories for such titles as* X-Men, Spider-Man, Fantastic Four, *and more. He is the co-creator of numerous iconic comic characters, including Red Sonja and Ghost Rider, and during his tenure at Marvel was directly responsible for bringing Conan the Barbarian to comic books.*

Lord of the Spiders

INTRODUCTION

"WE *MUST NOT* fail!" I looked up sharply. The speaker was a handsome giant of a man with burning, diamond-blue eyes. He was bending over one of the strangest devices I had ever seen. About the size of a telephone box, it was covered with dials and switches. A large coil suspended above it pulsed with power and on the right, in a dark corner, a dynamo of unusual design fed it with energy.

The tall man sat in a kind of cradle affair that was also suspended from the roof of the makeshift laboratory—really the cellars of my Belgravia house. I stood beneath the cradle, reading out to him the information given on the dials.

We had been at work on the machine for many weeks—or rather *he* had been at work. I had merely put up the money for the equipment he needed, and followed his instructions in doing the simple tasks he permitted me to do.

We had met fairly recently in France, where he had told me a strange and wild story about his adventures in—of all places—the planet Mars! There he had fallen in love with a beautiful princess of a city called Varnal of the Green Mists. He had fought against gigantic blue men called the Argzoon, finally succeeding in saving half a continent from their savage domination.

Put as baldly as this, the whole thing sounds like the paranoiac ravings of a madman or the lurid lies of a smooth-tongued taleteller. Yet I believed it—and still do.

I have already recounted this first meeting and what became of it—of how Michael Kane, the man who now worked in the cradle suspended above my head, had been a physicist in Chicago doing special research on something he called a "matter transmitter"; of how the early experiment had gone wrong and he had been transmitted not to another part of the lab, but *to Mars!*

It was a Mars, we believed, eons in the past, a Mars that thrived before Man ever walked this planet, a Mars of strange contrasts, customs, scenery—and beasts. A Mars of warring nations possessing the remnants of a once-mighty technical civilization—a Mars where Kane had come into his own. An expert swordsman, he had been a match for the master swordsmen of the Red Planet; a romantic despising his own dull environment, he had rejoiced at the luck which fate brought him.

But fate—in the guise of his fellow scientists—had also brought him back to Earth—back to here-and-now, just as he was about to marry his Martian sweetheart! The other scientists in Chicago had adjusted the fault in the transmitter and managed to recall Kane. One moment he had been sleeping in a Martian bed—the next he was back in the laboratory looking into the smiling faces of his fellow researchers! They thought they had done him a favour!

No one had believed his story. This brilliant scientist had been discredited when he had tried to convince the others that he had really been to Mars—a Mars that existed millions of years ago! He was not allowed near his own invention and he was given indefinite 'leave of absence.' Weighed down with despair of ever seeing his beloved Mars again, Kane had taken to wandering the world, aimlessly, thinking always of Vashu—the native name for Mars.

Then we had met by accident in a small café overlooking the French Mediterranean. He had told me the whole story. At the end of it I had agreed to help him build privately a transmitter similar to the one in Chicago so that, with luck, he would be able to return.

And now his device was almost ready!

"We must not fail!" He repeated the phrase, speaking half to himself as he worked with frowning concentration.

He would be taking his life in his hands if the experiment went wrong. He could have been flung through time and space at random the first time—he had only the flimsiest evidence to support his theory of spacio-temporal warp being affected by a special tuning of the transmitter, tuning which had existed during the first experiment. I had reminded him of this—that even if the transmitter worked there was scant likelihood of it sending him to Mars again. Even if it *did* send him to Mars, what chance was there of it being the same Mars of the time he had left?

But he held to his theory—a theory based, I felt, more upon what he wished than what actually was—and he placed all his faith on it working—*if* he picked the right time of year and day, and the right geographical position.

Apparently a spot near the city of Salisbury would be ideal—and tomorrow at eleven-thirty p.m. would be an excellent time. That was why we worked with such frantic haste.

So far as the actual equipment was concerned, I was sure it was all right. I did not pretend to understand his calculations but I trusted his character and his reputation as a physicist.

At last Kane looked away from the cone he'd been tinkering with and fixed me with that melancholy yet burning gaze with which I had become so familiar.

"That's it," he said. "There's nothing else we can do except ship it to our location. Is the power-wagon ready?"

"It is," I replied, referring to the transportable dynamo we would use to power his device. "Shall I phone the agency?"
He pursed his lips, frowning. He swung himself out of the cradle and dropped to the floor. He looked up at his brain-child and then his face relaxed. He seemed satisfied.

"Yes. Better phone them tonight rather than the morning." He nodded.

I went upstairs and put through a call to the employment agency, who were hiring us the 'muscle-power' we needed to get our equipment to its ultimate destination on Salisbury Plain. The men would be at my front door in the morning, the agency assured me.

When I returned I found Kane slumped in a chair, half asleep.

"Come along, old man," I said. "You'd better rest now or you'll be unable to do your best tomorrow."

He nodded mutely and I helped him upstairs to bed. Then I retired myself.

Next morning the men arrived with a large van. Under Kane's somewhat nervous supervision the matter-transmitter was taken out and secured inside the van.

Then we set off for Salisbury with me driving behind the larger vehicle in what Kane had chosen to call our power-wagon.

We had selected a spot not far from the famous Circle of Stones, Stonehenge. The great, primitive pillars—thought by many to be one of the earliest astronomical observatories—stood out boldly in the sharp light of early morning.

It was a restless day and the wind beat at the canvas of the tent as Kane and I worked to set up the equipment and give it a few tests to make sure it was working efficiently. This took us the best part of the day, and night was falling as I went to the van to switch on the dynamo in order to test the transmitter.

As the hours slipped by, Kane's face set more and more grimly. He was tense and kept reminding me of what I had to do when the time came. I knew it by heart—a simple business of checking certain instruments and pressing certain switches.

Shortly before eleven-thirty I went outside. The Moon was high, the night wild and stormy. Great banks of black cloud scudded across the sky. A night of portent!

I stood there smoking for a few minutes, huddled in my overcoat. My mind was half numb from the concentration of the previous weeks. Now that the experiment was about to take place I was almost afraid—afraid for Kane. He stood to lose if not his life, at least his hopes if we failed. And with the loss of hope, I felt, Kane would cease to be the man I admired.

He called to me from inside the tent.

When I went back I could see that his normal calmness was still not so apparent, partly due to his near-exhaustion, partly to his evident realization of the same things I had been thinking.

"We're almost ready, Edward."

I stamped out my cigarette and looked at the weird machine. The matter transmitter was alive now, humming with power. The scanner-cone at the top glowed a ruby red, giving the interior of the tent a bizarre appearance. Reflected in this glow, Kane's handsome face looked like that of some noble but unearthly demigod.

"Wish me luck." He smiled with an attempt at lightness. We shook hands.

He entered the transmitter and I closed the panel behind him, sealing it shut. I glanced at my watch. One minute to go. I dared not think—dared not consider, now, what I was about to do!

As the seconds ticked by I carefully recalled all his instructions, studied his instruments as needles quivered and dials glowed. I reached out my hand and depressed a button, flicked a switch. Simple actions, but actions which could either kill a man or consign him to limbo, either physical or mental.

There came a sudden, shrill note from above and the needles flickered frenetically. I knew what it meant.

Kane was on his way!

But where? When? Perhaps I would never know!

But now it was done. I walked slowly from the tent.

I lit another cigarette and smoked it. I thought about Kane, about his tales of high adventure and romance on an ancient planet. I wondered, as I had done before, if I had been right to believe him and help him. I wondered if I had been wrong.

Also I felt a loss—as if something strong and important had been removed from my life. I had lost a friend.

Then, suddenly, I heard a voice from within the tent!

With a shock I recognized Kane's voice—though now it had a different note to it.

So we had failed. Perhaps he had not gone anywhere. Perhaps his calculations had been wrong. Half in relief and half in trepidation, I stumbled back into the tent—to receive another shock!

The man who stood there was almost naked.

It was Kane—but not the Kane with whom I had shaken hands only minutes before.

I stared in astonishment at this apparition. It was clad in a leather harness of some sort, and it was decorated with strange, glowing gems which I could not recognize as any I knew. Across the broad, muscular shoulders was draped a light cloak of a wonderful blue colour. At its left hip the figure wore a long sword with a basket hilt—a sword suspended from a wide loop of thick leather but naked, unscabbarded. On his feet were heavy sandals laced up the calves to just below the knee. His hair, I now noticed, was longer, too. Upon his body were scars, some old and some fresh. He smiled strangely at me, as if greeting an old acquaintance from whom he had been separated for some time.

I recognized the gear from Kane's earlier descriptions. It was the gear of a *pakan*—a Warrior of Mars!

"Kane!" I gasped. "What has happened? Only a few moments ago you were..." I broke off, unable to speak, able only to stare!

He strode forward and grasped my shoulder in his powerful grip.

"Wait," he said firmly, "and I will explain. But first, can we return to your house in London? You might need that tape-recorder again!"

By means of the power-wagon we drove back to Belgravia, this strange, naked warrior with his long blade and alien, jeweled war-harness, sitting next to me.

Luckily we were unobserved as we entered my house. He moved lithely, his bronzed muscles rippling—a graceful super-man, a hero from the pages of Myth.

My housekeeper does not live in so I prepared him a meal myself and brought him some strong, black coffee which he seemed to relish a great deal.

I switched on the tape-recorder and he began to talk. Here is the tale he told me, edited only as to my questions and his asides—and some of the more secret scientific information—so as to present his own continuous narrative.

EDWARD P. BRADBURY,
Chester Square,
London, S.W.1.
April 1965

CHAPTER ONE
The Barren Plain

AFTER I HAD entered the matter transmitter I felt a tinge of fear. I realized fully for the first time just what I could lose.

But then it was too late. On your side of the transmitter you had done your work. I began to experience the familiar sensations associated with the machine. There was no difference save that this time I had no certainty of where I was going—you will remember that on my first trip I had thought I was merely being transmitted to a 'receiver' in another part of the laboratory building. Instead, I had been transported to my Mars. Now where was I bound? I prayed that it should be Mars again!

Strange colours spread themselves before my eyes. Again I felt weightless. There came a period during which I felt in communion with—everything. Then came the feeling of being bodiless, and yet hurtling through blackness at incredible velocities. My mind blanked out.

This time I awoke to comparative darkness. I lay face down on a hard, stony surface. I felt a little bruised, but not badly. I rolled over onto my back.

I was on Mars!

I knew it the moment I saw the twin moons—Urnoo and Garhoo in Martian, Phobos and Deimos in English—lighting a desolate landscape of chilly rocks and sparse vegetation. Over to the west something glinted—something that might have been a vast stretch of placid water.

I was still in the clothes I was wearing when I entered the transmitter. Its scanner broke down and translated into waveform everything placed inside the machine. I even had some loose change in my pockets, and my watch.

But something was wrong.

Gingerly I sat up. I was still a little dazed but already the suspicion was dawning on me that something had gone seriously wrong.

On my first two-way trip I had arrived just outside the city of Varnal on Southern Mars. And it was from Varnal that I had been snatched when my 'helpful' brother scientists drew me back to Earth.

But this wasteland was unlike any I had seen on *my* Mars!

Mars it was, of course—the moons proved that. Yet it did not seem to be the Mars of the age I had known—a Mars that had existed when dinosaurs still walked the Earth and Man had yet to come to dominance on my home planet.

I felt desperate, helpless, incredibly lonely. I had cut off all hope of ever seeing my beloved, betrothed Shizala again or of living in peace in the City of the Green Mists.

The Martian night is long and this seemed the longest of all until, when dawn began to appear, I finally rose and looked about me.

Nothing but sea and rock greeted my gaze whichever way I turned!

As I had guessed, I stood on a barren plain of brown-orange rock that stretched inland from a great, cold sea that moved slightly but restlessly, grey under a bleak sky.

Whether this was in the past or future of the Mars I knew I cared not. I only knew that if I was, as I suspected, on the exact geographical spot where once had stood—or once *would* stand— Varnal of the Green Mists and the Calling Hills, then all was lost to me! Now a sea rolled where the hills had rolled, rock occupied the place of the city.

I felt betrayed. It is difficult to describe why I should feel this. It was my own fault that I was here—and not even now embracing my sweetheart in the palace of the rulers of the Karnala.

I sighed, suddenly weary. Uncaring of what befell me, I began gloomily to walk inland. I had no purpose, it seemed, but to walk until I dropped from weariness and hunger. The barrenness of the landscape seemed to reflect the barrenness of ambition in myself.

All hope was dashed, all dreams vanished. Despair alone consumed me!

It was perhaps five hours—or approximately forty Martian *shatis*—later that I saw the beast. It must have been stalking me for some time.

The first thing I noticed about it was its weird, coruscating skin that caught the light and reflected it with all the colours of the rainbow. It was as if the beast were made of some kind of viscous, crystalline substance, but that was not so. Strange as it was, a second glance showed it to be of flesh and blood.

It was about eighteen to twenty *kilodas*—roughly six feet—high and thirty *kilodas* long. It was a powerful beast with a huge, wide mouth full of teeth that gleamed like crystal too. It had a single, many-faceted eye—an attribute of several Martian animals— and four short, heavily-muscled legs ending in big, clawed paws. It had no tail, but a kind of crest, perhaps of matted fur, oscillated along its back.

It was bent on having me for its lunch, that was clear.

Now my mood of despair left me as this danger threatened. I had no weapons, so I stooped and grabbed large rocks in each hand.

With an effort of will I faced the beast as it began to stalk slowly towards me, the crest oscillating quicker and quicker as if in anticipation of its meal. Yellowish saliva dripped from the open mouth and the single eye was fixed intently on me.

Suddenly I yelled and flung my first rock, aiming at the eye, following this shot with my second. The creature vented an incredible wailing cry, half of pain, half of anger. It reared on its hind legs and made lashing movements with its forelegs.

I picked up two more rocks and flung them at its soft underbelly. Evidently these did not have the same effect as those I had hurled at the eye. The beast dropped to all fours again and held its ground—as I held mine—regarding me balefully.

It seemed to be stalemate for the moment.

Slowly I stooped and felt around for more ammunition. I found one rock—there were no more.

Now the crest trembled and fluttered, the mouth opened still wider and the drooling increased. Then the creature took several steps backward but I could tell it was not retreating and was merely preparing to spring.

I tried a trick which I knew had worked on Earth when men had been in a similar position confronted by wild beasts. I shouted at the top of my voice and ran towards it, the hand holding the rock upraised.

I ran full tilt almost into its horrid maw.

The beast had not moved an inch!

Now I was in worse straits than I was before!

Deciding to sell my life dearly, I flung my last rock at the eye and dashed past to get behind it. The beast screamed, wailed and reared again. Then I saw thick blood beginning to ooze down its muzzle. It scuttled round, still on its hind legs, forelegs waving, claws slashing at air. I had hit the lower part of the eye. I must have inflicted some damage, for the blood was evident, but the beast could still see.

I stooped towards another rock and then, with a speed I had not expected, it was dashing towards me, jaws gaping!

I flung myself out of its path just in time—but already it was whirling round and coming at me again. I knew I hadn't a chance.

I remember lying on the rock trying to turn over and get to my feet, fearfully aware of that great bulk rushing down on me, the shining teeth, the saliva...

And then, only inches from me, the beast fell to the ground, threshed and was still.

What had happened? I thought at first that my rock must have done more damage than I had suspected, but when I got up I saw a long, heavy lance jutting from the beast's side.

I looked around, saw the figure standing there—and was instantly on my guard again. This was a Blue Giant—an Argzoon. I had previously experienced their savagery—I knew they attacked men such as me on sight.

The Argzoon was well armed, with sword and mace at left and right hips. He was magnificently muscled and almost ten feet tall.

What confirmed my suspicion that I was in a different era was the fact that instead of wearing the normal Argzoon leather breastplate his was of fine metal, as were his wristguards and greaves.

Perhaps he had saved my life in order to have some sport with me. I began attempting to wrench his lance from the corpse of the beast so that I would have something with which to defend myself when he attacked.

I got the lance free as he came close. He smiled and stood regarding me with some puzzlement in his manner, arms akimbo, head slightly to one side.

"I am ready for you, Argzoon," I said in Martian.

He laughed then—not the savage, animal laugh of the Argzoon but a good-humoured laugh. Had the Argzoon changed so much?

"I saw your fight with the *rhadari*," he said. "You are very brave."

Warily I lowered the lance, saying nothing. The voice, too, had been unlike the Argzoon guttural which I knew.

He pointed at me, smiling again. "Why are you swathed in that bulky cloth? Are you ill?"

I shook my head, feeling a little embarrassed already, both by my appearance—which was odd on Mars, to say the least—and my assumption that he was a foe.

"I am called Hool Haji," he said. "Your name and tribe?"

"Michael Kane," I said, finding my tongue at last. "I have no native tribe, but am an adopted member of the Karnala nation."

"A strange name—but I know of the Karnala. By reputation, they are as brave as you have shown yourself to be."

"You'll pardon me," I said, "but you do not seem typical of the Argzoon nation."

He laughed good-humouredly. "Thank you. That is because I am of the Mendishar."

I seemed to have heard vaguely of the Mendishar, but could not remember what I had been told—by Shizala probably, I thought.

"Is this Mendishar?" I asked.

"I wish it were. We are nearly there, however."

"Where is Mendishar in relation to Argzoon?"

"Oh, we lie well to the north of the Caves of Darkness."

The discrepancy in time could not be as great as I had at first thought, then. If the Karnala and the Argzoon's underground world, the Caves of Darkness, still existed, then the spot—this barren waste—on which I had found myself was not typical of the planet I knew.

Hool Haji reached out his hand. "Perhaps I could have my lance now?"

I apologized and handed it to him.

"You look exhausted," he said. "Come—I have a camp nearby— we'll eat a little of your late adversary." He bent down and lifted the great beast's carcase easily, flinging it over his shoulder.

I walked beside him and he deliberately shortened his pace so that I might find it easier to keep up with him. He did not seem to tire beneath his burden.

"I was graceless," I said. "I did not thank you for saving my life. I am in your debt."

"May you have an opportunity to repay it," he replied, using a formal reply which I had only heard in the south until now.

We reached Hool Haji's camp—a low tent pitched beside a small stream that ran through the rocks. A fire was burning and giving off a great deal of ill-smelling smoke, but Hool Haji explained that the only fuel in these parts was in the *oxel*, the brownish, bracken-like plant that sprouted among the rocks.

Hool Haji began to skin the beast and as he did so, preparing it most deftly with a special knife he wore in his upper harness, he explained the similarities between his race and the Argzoon. I was interested to hear it, especially since it also told me a little more about the earlier history of Vashu—or Mars, as they call it on Earth.

It seems that in the dim and distant past of Vashu the Mendishar and the Argzoon were one people, living close to the sea from which, their legends said, they had originated. They were fishermen and boat builders, pirates and coastal raiders, sea traders, *inrak* divers—the inrak being a rare shell-fish regarding as a delicacy by all, it appeared, but the blue men themselves.

They lived in a part of the planet which at that time was remote. Their lives were parochial, their trading and raiding confined mostly to nearby places.

Then came the Mightiest War. About the cause of this war and its protagonists Hool Haji was rather vague. It was between the Sheev and the Yaksha, he said. I had heard of the Sheev. This mysterious people had given many benefits to the Karnala—they had once possessed a great civilization, understood nuclear energy and the like, were more advanced than Earthmen of my own time. The ruins of their cities were still sometimes to be found here and there. Hool Haji appeared to know little more than I did. The Yaksha and the Sheev were of similar origins, he said, but the Yaksha were considerably less wholesome.

The Mightiest War was waged across the planet for decades. Soon even the remote blue men heard of it. Soon they even suffered from its effects, many dying from the strange disease borne on the wind from the west.

Then the Yaksha came to the settlements of the blue folk. They had many wonderful weapons, but they seemed beaten and desperate. The handful of Yaksha offered the blue men great chances of plunder if they would help them attack a Sheev position inland. Many had agreed and had set off for the mountains where the Sheev were. Apparently they had found the Sheev in underground chambers blasted from the rock, and had attacked. The Sheev had held them off until only three of the Sheev survived. Then these had escaped in a flying boat of some kind. The Yaksha, also few in number, had followed them, telling the blue folk to hold the position until they returned.

They had not returned. The blue folk settled in the cavernworld. Some had brought women. They adapted to the environment and had even seemed to thrive on it. The caverns were an ideal place from which to conduct raids on the smaller, lighter-skinned races—so they had raided. That had been the origin of the Argzoon millennia before.

The Mendishar were those who had remained. They had taken no part in the Mightiest War, but had prospered, trading amongst far islands and a continent which lay beyond the sea to the north.

"That is," Hool Haji said as he set the meat on a spit over the fire, "until the Priosa gained too much power."

"Who are they?" I asked.

"Originally they were simply a royal guard—a ceremonial force attached to our Bradhi's house." A Bradhi was a kind of Martian king who tended to rule by heredity but could be deposed and replaced by popular vote. "They were made up of young warriors who had won honour among our people. They were idolized by the populace who began, by degrees, to attach an almost mystical significance to them. In the minds of the ordinary folk they became more then men, almost deities—they could do what they liked virtually with impunity. Then, about forty years ago, the warrior who was then Pukan Nara"—this meant, roughly, Warrior-leader—"of the Priosa began to say that he was receiving messages from higher beings.

"Realizing that the whole system of the Priosa offered a danger to the Mendishar nation, the Bradhi and his council decided to disband it. But they had reckoned without the power the Priosa now held over the ordinary folk. When they announced the decision to disband the force the people refused to hear of it. The Bradhi was deposed and the Pukan Nara—Jewar Baru—was elected Bradhi. The old Bradhi and his council all died mysteriously in different ways, the Bradhi's family was forced to flee and the new Bradhi Jewar Baru began his unhealthy reign."

"In what way is it unhealthy?" I asked.

"They have brought superstition back into the lives of the Mendishar. They perform 'miracles' and claim clairvoyance; they receive 'messages' from 'higher beings'... it is religion debased to its lowest level."

I knew the pattern. It was not unlike similar episodes in my own planet's chequered history.

"They are now a caste of warrior-priests milking the nation of its riches," Hool Haji continued, "to the point where many are now disillusioned. But Jewar Baru and his 'more-than-men' have total power and those who are disillusioned and say so publicly soon find themselves taking part in one of their barbaric ritual sacrifices where a man's—or a woman's—heart is torn out in the central square of Mendisharling, our nation's capital city."

I was disgusted. "But what part do you play in this?" I asked him.

"An important one," he said. "A rebellion is planned and many rebels wait in the small hill villages beyond Mendisharling. They need only a leader to unite under and march against the Priosa."

"And that leader is not forthcoming?"

"I am that leader," he said. "I hope their faith in me will be justified. I am the last of the line of the old Bradhis—my father was slain on Jewar Baru's orders. My family wandered the wastelands, seeking refuge and finding none, hunted by bands of Priosa. Those who were not killed by the Priosa died of malnutrition and disease, of attacks by wild beasts such as our friend there." He pointed at the carcase which was now beginning to roast well.

"At length only I, Hool Haji, remained. Though I yearned for Mendishar I could think of no way of returning—until a messenger found me wandering, many days' journey from this spot, and told me of the rebels, of their longing for a leader, how as last of the old line I would be ideal. I agreed to go to the hill village he told me of—and I am now on my way."

"Since I have no aims," I said, "perhaps you will allow me to accompany you."

"Your presence will be welcome. I am a lonely man."

We ate and I told him my story, which he did not find as incredible as I had suspected he would.

"We are used to strange happenings on Vashu," he said. "From time to time the shadows of the older races pass across us in the form of rediscovered marvels, strange inventions of which we know little. Your story is unusual—but possible. Everything is possible."

I realized once again that the Martians are a philosophical folk on the whole—somewhat fatalistic in our terms, I suppose, yet with a strong tradition and moral code that save them from any hint of decadence.

After our meal we slept, and it was night again by the time we set off for the hills of Mendishar.

Dawn rose on those hills which marked the border of the Mendishar nation, and Hool Haji had to restrain himself from lengthening his steps.

It was as we set foot on blue-green sward that two riders, mounted on the huge, ape-like daharas, riding beasts of almost all Martian nations, topped the nearest hill, paused for a moment when they saw us and then rode full tilt at us.

They were gaudily dressed, with brightly lacquered armour and long, coloured plumes in close-fitting helmets. Their swords flashed in the early morning sun.

They were clearly bent on taking our lives!

Hool Haji cried one word as he flung me his long lance and drew his sword.

That word was—"Priosa!"

The pair thundered down on us and I held my lance ready as my opponent's great sword swung up, preparing to crash down and cleave my skull.

It swept towards me. I deflected it with my lance but the force of his blow knocked my weapon from my hands and I was forced to leap out of the warrior's path, dashing to retrieve the lance as he wheeled his mount and grinned with narrowed eyes, sure of an easy victory.

CHAPTER TWO
Ora Lis

THE GIANT BLUE warrior now aimed his sword at me as if to impale me—I was sure that was his intention.

My lance was only a short distance from me but there was no time to pick it up. When the point of his sword was almost at my throat I flung myself backwards, feeling the metal literally part my hair! Then I grabbed for the lance and leapt to my feet.

He was once again turning his mount when I saw my opportunity and hurled my lance at him.

It took him in the face and killed him instantly. He fell back, the lance quivering in his head. His sword dropped from his hand and hung by its wrist thong. The unruly dahara reared up, sensing that its master no longer controlled it, and the corpse toppled from the saddle.

Glancing about me, I saw that Hool Haji had not had my luck—for luck it had been. He was defending himself from a rain of blows his attacker was aiming at him. He had dropped to one knee.

Snatching up my late opponent's sword, I ran forward with a yell. I must have looked a peculiar sight, still in jacket, shirt and trousers, armed with a huge blade, running to the aid of one of two battling blue giants!

Foolishly, Hool Haji's antagonist half-turned at my yell. My blue ally needed only that momentary diversion. He sprang up, knocked aside his opponent's weapon and plunged his sword into the Priosa's throat.

The giant was scarcely dead before Hool Haji was grasping the dahara's harness and steadying the beast as its late master fell sideways from the saddle. Somewhat contemptuously, the ex-Bradhinak freed the feet of the corpse from the stirrups and let it drop to the ground.

I realized what my friend had in mind and turned towards the other dahara, which had moved a short distance away and was nervously looking about. Without its rider it looked even more curiously manlike than ever. The dahara was descended from the common ape-ancestor of Man. If anyone had said of it, as is sometimes said of dogs and horses on Earth, that it was 'almost human,' that person would have stated a plain fact! Their intelligence varied according to species, the intelligence of the smaller Southern variety being greater than that of this much larger Northern variety. I approached the big dahara with caution, talking to it soothingly. It shied away—but not before I was able to catch its reins. It made a token snap at me—I have never known even the wildest dahara to attack a man—and then it was under my control.

Now we both had mounts and enough weapons to arm me.

A trifle ghoulishly, we stripped the corpses of everything we needed—but it was a pity that the armour fitted neither of us, Hool Haji being a little too large and I a lot too small, but I was able to make a crossbelt to go over my shoulders and take the heavy weapons. I was also, thankfully, able to rid myself of the greater part of my encumbering Earthly clothing. Feeling more like a warrior of Mars with my weapons strapped about me and seated on the broad back of the dahara, I galloped along, keeping pace with Hool Haji as we headed once more into the hills.

Now we were at last at Mendishar. The village—called Asde-Trahi—lay only a few miles away.

We soon reached it. I had expected something more primitive than the bright, mosaic walls of the low, semi-spherical houses—many of the mosaics being arranged as pictures, very beautiful and artistic. The village was surrounded by a wall, though as we rode down the hill towards it we could see the whole of the interior. The wall was also decorated, but in paints of strong, primary colours—orange, blue and yellow—with geometrical designs mainly based on the circle and the rectangle.

As we neared Asde-Trahi, figures began to appear on the walls. The figures were almost all armed and their weapons were drawn. These were blue giants, but their armour, if they wore it at all, was of padded leather similar to that which the Argzoon, my old enemies, wore. Their weapons, too, seemed to be whatever they had been able to lay hands on.

When we were closer, one of the figures gave out a wild yell and began to talk rapidly to his companions.

A great cheer rang out then and the warriors held their swords and axes high, leaping up and down in exultation.

Evidently Hool Haji had been recognized and was welcome.

From a flag-mast in the center of the village one banner was run down and another raised. I gathered they were literally raising the flag of rebellion. The heavy yellow and black square banner was apparently the old standard of the deposed Bradhis.

Hool Haji smiled at me as the gates opened in the wall.

"It is a homecoming worth waiting for," he said.

We rode into the village and men and women and the Mendishar children—some of them were almost my own height!—flocked around Hool Haji, their voices babbling their welcome.

One of the women—I suppose she was beautiful by their standards—clung to Hool Haji's arm and looked with large eyes up into his face.

"I have waited so long for you, great Bradhinak," I heard her say. "I have dreamed of this day."

Hool Haji seemed rather embarrassed—as I'd had been—and had some difficulty disengaging his arm from the woman's embrace, but was able to do so when he saw a tall, dignified young warrior come towards him, hands outstretched in welcome.

"Morahi Vaja!" the exile exclaimed in pleasure. "You see, I kept my promise."

"And I mine," smiled the young warrior. "There is not a village in these hills that does not willingly offer its support to you and our cause."

The woman was still there, though she no longer embraced Hool Haji.

Morahi Vaja stepped towards her. "This is my sister, Ora Lis— she has never met you, but she is already your greatest supporter." Morahi Vaja smiled. Then he spoke to the girl. "Ora Lis, will you instruct the servants to prepare Hool Haji's friend a bed and food?" The young warrior seemed not at all surprised by the appearance of a stranger—a stranger of a different race, at that—in his village.

Hool Haji realized it was time to introduce me. "This is Michael Kane—he is from Negalu," he said, using the Martian name for the planet Earth.

This time Morahi Vaja did show slight surprise. "I thought Negalu was inhabited only by giant reptiles and the like," he said.

Hool Haji laughed. "He is not only from Negalu—he is from the future!"

Morahi Vaja smiled a little. "Well then, greetings, friend—I hope you bring luck to our enterprise."

I restrained myself from remarking that I hoped I could since I had brought little to my own!

As we dismounted, Hool Haji said: "Michael Kane saved my life when we were attacked by Priosa earlier today."

"You are welcome and honoured," Morahi Vaja said to me.

"Hool Haji forgets to tell you that he saved mine before I saved his," I pointed out as Morahi Vaja led us towards a large house decorated in the most splendid mosaics I have ever seen.

"Then it was ordained that he should—for if you had not been saved you could not have saved him."

I could think of no reply to such logic. We entered the house. It was cool and the rooms were large, light and simply decorated.

Ora Lis was already there. She had eyes only for Hool Haji, who seemed both slightly flattered and embarrassed by her attention.

Morahi Vaja was plainly a person of some consequence in the village—he was, it emerged later, a kind of mayor—and we were given the best of everything. The food and drink were delicious, though some of it was plainly produced only in the North, since it was unfamiliar to me.

We ate and drank our fill and all the while Ora Lis paid Hool Haji every attention, even begging to be allowed to remain when Morahi Vaja told her we were now to talk of strategy and logistics.

The reasons for the planned rebellion were twofold. One, the people were beginning to realize that the Priosa were by no means superior beings—too many daughters and matrons had testified to the fact that the Priosa's appetites were scarcely those of enlightened demigods—and two, the Priosa were becoming more lax, more self-indulgent, less inclined to ride out on their patrols.

It seemed to me that this process was not unfamiliar—it seems to be something of a law of nature that the tyrant falls by his own lack of foresight. It has always been that the wise king, no matter what kind of character he may possess, protects his subjects and thereby protects himself. The larger and more complex the society, the longer the process of disposing of the tyrant. Often, of course, one tyrant is substituted for another and a vicious circle is brought about. In the end, however, this means the destruction of the state—its conquest or decline—and sooner or later the enlightened ruler or government will arise. This may take centuries—or a few weeks—and it is, of course, hard to be philosophical when it is your face that is beneath the iron heel.

We talked into the night and I was sometimes amused to see Hool Haji having to refuse a dish of fruit or the offer of another cushion from the attentive Ora Lis.

Our plan was based on the belief that, once a large force of village-living Mendishar attacked the capital city, the townsfolk would join them.

It seemed logical that this would be so. Everything seemed ripe.

It had not been thus not so long ago, Morahi Vaja informed us. The men of the villages and small towns had been wary of following Morahi Vaja, who was, in their eyes, too young and untried. But when he had been able to contact Hool Haji everything had changed. Now they were enthusiastic.

"You are very valuable, Bradhi," said Morahi Vaja. "You must protect yourself until the time for the rising, for if we were to lose you we should lose our whole cause!"

Hool Haji made some self-depreciating remark, but Morahi Vaja's face was very serious. Evidently he meant what he said—and knew that what he said was true!

We were given a room each in Morahi Vaja's house. My bed was the plain, unsprung bed that predominates all over Mars. I was soon asleep.

I had gone to bed in a mixed mood of desolation and anticipation. It was not so easy to forget, even for a moment or two, that I was separated from the woman I loved by barriers impossible to cross. On the other hand, the cause of the tyrannized folk of Mendishar was one close to my heart. We Americans always have sympathy with the oppressed, whoever they may be, so long as they themselves are fighting back. Not a very Christian attitude, perhaps, but one which I share with most of my countrymen and probably with most of humanity.

I awoke in a somewhat more philosophical frame of mind. There was hope—faint hope. You remember that I told you of the wonderful inventions of the mysterious Sheev? Well, that was my hope—that some time I might contact the Sheev and ask them for help in crossing time and space once again—this time not from planet to planet but from one time and place on Mars to another.

I resolved to seek out the Sheev—or a member of the race—as soon as I had seen the revolution of Mendishar successful. I felt involved in it, principally because I regarded Hool Haji as a close friend, and anything he did was of interest to me.

A light tap on my door came soon after I had awakened. Sunlight was streaming through the unglazed window and there was a sweet, fresh smell in the air—the familiar scents of the Martian countryside.

I called for the person outside to enter. It was a female servant—the blue females are only a foot or two shorter than the males—with a tray of hot food. This in itself was a surprise, for the Southern Martian breakfast usually consists of fruit and the like.

While I was finishing the breakfast Hool Haji came in. He was smiling. After greeting me he sat on the bed and burst out laughing.

His laugher was infectious and I found myself smiling in response, though I did not know the cause of his mirth.

"What is it?" I asked.

"That woman," he said, still grinning. "Morahi Vaja's sister—what's her name?"

"Ora Lis?"

"That's right. Well, she brought me my breakfast this morning."

"Is that strange?"

"It is very courteous—though a rare custom amongst our people. It was not so much the action, which I should normally have accepted as a compliment, as what she said."

"What did she say?" I had a feeling of unease then. As I have mentioned before, I seem to be slightly psychic—or whatever you care to call it. I have some sixth sense which warns me of trouble. Some would call it the logic of the subconscious which accumulates and draws conclusions from data which never reaches the conscious mind.

"In short," declared my friend, "she told me that she knew our destinies to be intertwined. I believe she thinks I am going to marry her."

"Ah, infatuation," I said, still somewhat perturbed, nonetheless. "You are the mysterious exile returned to claim a throne, and what could be more romantic than that? What girl would not respond to it? It is not an uncommon feeling, I have heard."

He nodded. "Yes, yes. That is why I did not treat the declaration too seriously. I was polite enough to her, never fear."

I fingered my chin thoughtfully, realizing suddenly that I had not shaved for some time—there was a heavy stubble there. I would do something about it soon. "What did you say?" I asked.

"I told her that the business of the revolt was consuming all my attention, that I had noticed she was beautiful... She is, don't you think?"

I did not answer this. All beauty is comparative, I know, but I could not, frankly, tell a beautiful, eight-foot, blue giantess from an ugly one!

"I told her that we should have to wait before we could become better acquainted," the Mendishar continued, chuckling.

I felt slightly relieved by the knowledge that my friend had behaved so tactfully.

"A wise thing to say." I nodded. "When you sit the throne of Mendishar as Bradhi, that will be the time to think of romance—or the avoiding of it."

"Exactly," said Hool Haji, bringing his great bulk to a standing position once more. "I don't quite know if she accepted this. She seemed to take it rather as a declaration of my own passion, which troubled me a little."

"Do not worry," I said. "What are your plans for today?"

"We must work speedily and prepare a message to be sent to all the *cilaks* and *orcilaks* calling them to a full-scale meeting here." The two Martian words meant, roughly, village-leader and town-leader, the suffix *ak* designating one holding power over his fellows or—strictly speaking, in Martian, one who was charged by his fellows to act in their interests. *Cil* meant a small community, *orcil* meant a larger one.

"This is necessary," Hool Haji continued, "in order that they should see for themselves that I am who I am as well, of course, as deciding when and how we shall strike and deploy our warriors."

"How many warriors do you estimate having at your disposal?" I enquired washing myself with the cold water provided.

"About ten thousand."

"And how many Priosa will they have to contend with?"

"About five thousand, including the warriors not of the Priosa but expected to support them. The Priosa will, of course, be much better armed and trained. My people have a habit of fighting independently of any command. The Priosa have rid themselves of this lack of discipline, but I am not sure if the same can be said for many of the village-dwelling warriors."

I understood. This was a trait which the Mendishar shared with their Argzoon cousins. The Argzoon had only been united under that arch-villainess Horguhl—and united largely through fear of a common enemy, the N'aal Beast, and superstition.

"That is another reason why my presence is needed," said Hool Haji. "They will, Morahi Vaja feels, fight under an hereditary Bradhi, whereas they would be disinclined to take orders from a mere *cilak*."

"Then Morahi Vaja was right—you are invaluable to the cause."

"It seems so. It is a great responsibility."

"It is responsibility to which you will have to become accustomed," I told him. "As Bradhi of Mendishar you will have heavy responsibilities for your people all your life."

He sighed and gave me a wry smile. "There are some advantages in being a lone wanderer in the wilderness, are there not?"

"There are. But if you are of royal blood you are not free to choose."

He sighed again and gripped the hilt of this great sword. "You are more than an able fighting companion, Michael Kane. You are also a friend of strong character."

I grasped his arm and looked up into his eyes. "Those words apply to you, Bradhinak Hool Haji."

"I hope so," he said.

CHAPTER THREE

Hool Haji's Duty

A FEW DAYS later we received word that all the various leaders of the towns and villages had been given secret word and a great meeting was planned in three days' time.

During that period of waiting we had spent long hours in planning and fewer hours in relaxation. Hool Haji spent a great deal of the time with Ora Lis. Like any man, he was flattered by her adoration and could not resist basking in it. I felt that no good could come of this, but I could not blame him. In circumstances other then mine I might have done the same myself. In fact, I have done it myself more than once in the past, though not nearly so much was at stake then.

It seemed to me that Ora Lis was given good cause to think that her passion was being reciprocated, but I could find no way of warning my friend.

Once I found myself in the same room with her, alone, and I talked with her for a short time.

In spite of what was, to me, her outlandish size and strange face, she was plainly a simple, ingenuous, romantic girl. I tried to speak of Hool Haji, told her of his many obligations to his people, that it might be years before he could think of himself—and the taking of a wife.

Her response to this was to laugh and shrug her shoulders.

"You are a wise man, Michael Kane—my brother says that your counsel has aided them greatly—but I think you are not so wise in matters of love."

This struck deeper than it should have done, for thoughts of my own love, Shizala, were forever with me. But I persevered.

"Have you not thought that Hook Haji may not feel so strongly about you as you do for him?" I asked gently.

Again the smile and the light laugh. "We are to be married in two days' time," she told me.

I gasped. "Married? Hool Haji has told me nothing of this!"

"Has he not? Well, it is so, nonetheless!"

After that I could make no reply but resolved to seek out Hool Haji at the earliest opportunity.

I found him standing on the north wall of the village, looking out over the lovely, blue-green hills, the cultivated fields that sustained the villagers, and the large, scarlet rhani flowers that grew in profusion hereabouts.

"Hool Haji," I said without preliminary, "did you know that Ora Lis thinks she is to marry you in two days' time?"

He turned, smiling. "Is that it? She is living out some fantasy in a world of her own, I fear. She told me mysteriously yesterday that if I met her by a certain tree yonder"—he pointed to the north-east—"that which we both desired would be brought about. A secret marriage! Even more romantic than I guessed."

"But do you not realize that she sincerely believes you intend to make the rendezvous?"

He drew a deep breath. "Yes, I suppose so. I must do something about it, mustn't I?"

"You must—and swiftly. The poor girl!"

"You know, Michael Kane, the duties of the past days have left me in a state almost of euphoria. I have spent time in Ora Lis' company because I found it the most relaxing thing I could do. Yet I have hardly heard anything she has said to me—can remember scarcely a word I have said to her. Plainly, things have gone too far."

The sun was beginning to set, staining the deep blue sky with veins of red, yellow and purple.

"Will you go to see her now?" I described where she was.

He yawned wearily. "No—I had best do it when I am more refreshed. In the morning."

We walked back slowly to the house of our host. We passed Ora Lis on our way. She went swiftly by, pausing only to give Hool Haji a secret smile.

I was horrified. I understood my friend's predicament, how the situation must have arisen, and I could sympathize with him. Now we had to do what every man hates to do—put a girl into the deepest possible misery in the most tactful possible way. Knowing something of these situations, I also knew that, no matter how tactful a man ties to be, something always results so that he is misunderstood and the girl weeps, refusing to be comforted by him. Few women do not respond in this manner—and, frankly, those are the ones I admire—women like my own Shizala, who was as feminine as could be but with a will of iron and a strength of character most men would envy.

Not that I did not sympathize with the poor Ora Lis. I sympathized very much. She was young, innocent—a village-girl with none of the unpretentious sophistication of my Shizala, and none of the rigid training that all members of the Southern Martian royal houses receive.

I sympathized with both. But it was up to Hool Haji to do his unpleasant duty. And I knew that he would.

Again, after I had bathed and shaved with a specially honed knife I had borrowed from Morahi Vaja—the blue Martians have no body hair to speak of—and climbed wearily into bed, I was filled with a sense of deep disquiet that would not leave me even in sleep. I tossed and turned throughout the long Martian night and in the morning felt as unrefreshed as when I had gone to bed.

Having risen and splashed cold water all over my body in an effort to rid myself of my feeling of tiredness, I ate the food the servant had brought me, strapped on my weapons and went out into the courtyard of the house.

It was a beautiful morning but I could not appreciate it greatly.

Just as I was turning back to look for Hool Haji, Ora Lis came flying from the house. Tears ran freely down her face and great groaning sobs came from her.

I realized that Hool Haji must have spoken to her and told her the truth—the unpalatable truth. I tried to speak to her, to say some comforting words to her, but she was past me in a flash and running into the street.

I told myself that it was best that it should have happened this way and that, being young and resilient, the poor girl would soon recover from her misery and find another young warrior upon whom she could lavish the passion that was so plainly part of her character.

But I was wrong. I was to be proved very wrong in the events which followed.

Hool Haji came out of the house next. He walked slowly, with head bowed. When he looked up and saw me, I noticed that his eyes reflected pain and sadness.

"You have done it," I said.

"Yes."

"I saw her—she ran past me and would not stop when I called to her. It was the best thing."

"I suppose so."

"She will soon find someone else," I said.

"You know, Michael Kane," he said with a sigh, "it cost me more than you realize to do what I did. In other circumstances I might have grown to love Ora Lis."

"Perhaps you will when this is over."

"Will it not then be too late?"

I had to be realistic. "Possibly," I told him.

He seemed to make an effort to dismiss the thoughts from his mind. "Come," he said, "we must speak with Morahi Vaja. He would learn your views on the deploying of the axe-men from Sala-Ras."

If Hool Haji was in a mood of depression, I was in one of utmost foreboding.

More was going to come out of this episode than either of us could have foreseen.

It was to change the entire course of events and fling me into some strange adventures.

It was to mean death to many.

CHAPTER FOUR

Betrayed!

THE DAY OF the great meeting dawned and Ora Lis had not returned. Nor had the search parties that had gone seeking her discovered a trace of her. We all became worried, but priority had to be given to the meeting.

The proud cilaks and orcilaks were arriving. They had travelled secretly and always alone. The Priosa patrols were ever wary for large groups of men who might represent danger.

Farmers, merchants, artisans, dahara trainers, whatever their normal occupations they were all warriors. Even the Priosa tyranny had not been able to forbid the countrymen to give up their right to bear arms. And armed they were—to the teeth.

Guards were stationed in the surrounding hills to keep a lookout for any Priosa patrol, though none was expected on this particular day, which was why the meeting had been called now.

There were more than forty village-leaders and town-leaders there, all of them looking eminently trustworthy and with integrity ingrained in their faces. But there was independence too—the kind of independence that would prefer to fight its own battles and not rely on any group effort. Their habitual looks of suspicion changed somewhat, however, as soon as they entered the big room set aside for the meeting in Morahi Vaja's house. They saw Hool Haji there and they said, "He is like the old Bradhinak alive again!" And that was enough. There was no bowing of the knee or servile salute—they held themselves straight. But there was a new air of determination about them now.

Having ascertained that all were convinced of Hool Haji's identity, Morahi Vaja unrolled a large map of Mendishar and hung it on the wall behind him. He outlined our basic strategy and proposed tactics in certain conditions. The local leaders asked questions—very thoughtful and penetrating ones—and we answered them. Whenever we could not answer at once we discussed it.

With men like these, I realized, pitched against the unwary Priosa, it would be no difficult feat to win the capital and wrest Jewar Baru's stolen power away from him.

But still the feeling of disquiet was with me. I could not shift it. I was constantly on my guard, glancing about me warily, my hand on my sword.

A meal was brought into the hall at midday and we ate as we talked, for there was no time to lose.

By early afternoon the initial talking was over and smaller details were being discussed—how best to use certain small groups of men with a special fighting-skill, how to use individuals such as the local champion spearmen, and so on.

By dusk most of us were satisfied that on the day set for the attack—in another three days—we should be ready and we should win!

But we were never to make that attack.

Instead, at sunset, we were attacked!

They came on the village from all sides and we were hopelessly outnumbered and out-weaponed.

They came in a charge, mounted on daharas, their armour shining in the dying sunlight, their plumes waving and their lances, shields, swords, maces and axes flashing.

The noise was terrible, for it was the baying bloodlust of men prepared—no, enjoying the prospect—to wipe out a village, man, woman and child.

It was the cry of the wolverine debased in a human throat.

It was a cry not only to strike terror into the hearts of the women and children, but into the hearts of grown, brave men. It was a cry that was merciless, malevolent, already triumphant.

It was the cry of the human hunter of the human prey!

We saw them riding through the streets, striking at anything that moved. The cruel glee on their faces was indescribable. I saw a woman die clutching her child. Her head was sliced off and the child impaled on a lance. I saw a man try to defend himself against the battering weapons of four riders—and go down with a shriek of rage and hatred.

It was a nightmare.

How had this come about? We had been betrayed, that was plain. These were the Priosa, unmistakably.

We rushed into the streets, standing shoulder to shoulder and taking the savage riders as they came at us.

It was the end of everything. With us dead the people would be leaderless. Even if some escaped, there would not be enough to launch any sizable revolt.

Who had betrayed us?

I could think of no one. Certainly not one of these village-leaders, men of pride and integrity, who were even now falling before the weight of the Priosa attack.

Night fell as we fought—but darkness did not, for the scene was illuminated by the houses which the attackers had already set ablaze.

If I had had any doubts that Hool Haji had exaggerated the cruelty of the tyrant and his chosen supporters they were quickly dismissed. I have never seen such sadism exhibited by one part of a race for another.

Memory of it is still burned deep in my mind. I shall never forget that night of terror—I wish that I could.

We fought until our bodies ached. One by one the brave hope of Mendishar fell in their own blood, but not before they had taken many of the better-equipped Mendishar with them!

I met steel with steel. My movements became almost mechanical—defence and attack, block a thrust or a blow, deflect it, aim a thrust or a blow of my own. I felt like a machine. The events, the weariness, had momentarily driven all emotion from me.

It was later, when only a few of us remained, that I became aware of a shouted conversation between Hool Haji and Morahi Vaja, who stood to my left.

Morahi Vaja was remonstrating with my friend, telling him to flee. But Hool Haji refused to go.

"You must go—it is your duty!"

"Duty! It is my duty to fight with my people!"

"It is your duty to choose exile again. You are our only hope. If you are killed or captured tonight, then the whole cause is destroyed. Leave, and there will come others to take the place of those who have died tonight."

I at once saw the logic of what Morahi Vaja said and added my voice to his.

We continued to fight, arguing as we did so. It was a bizarre scene!

Eventually Hool Haji realized that this must be so—that he must leave.

"But you must come with me, Michael Kane. I—I shall need you comfort and your advice."

Poor devil—he was in a strange mood and might do something rash. I agreed.

Pace by pace we retreated to where two men, grimfaced, held mounts for us.

We were soon riding out of the devastated village, but we knew that Priosa would be encircling the place waiting for such an attempt—it was a standard tactic.

I glanced back and again felt horror!

A small group of defenders stood shoulder to shoulder just outside Morahi Vaja's house. Everywhere else were the dead—dead of both sexes and of all ages. Lurid flames licked from the once beautiful mosaic houses. It was a scene from Bosch or Breughel—a picture of hell.

Then I was forced to turn my attention to the sound of dahara feet thundering towards us.

I am not a man to hate easily—but those Priosa I hated.

I welcomed the opportunity to kill the three who came at us, grinning.

We used warm, much-bloodied steel to wipe those grins from their faces.

Then we rode on, heavy-hearted, away from that place of anger and cruelty.

We rode until it was almost impossible to keep our eyes open and the cold morning came.

It was then that we saw the remains of a camp and the outline of a prone figure stretched on the sward.

As we neared the camp we recognized the figure.

It was Ora Lis.

With a cry of surprise, Hool Haji rode up to the spot and dismounted, kneeling beside the woman. As I joined him I saw that Ora Lis was wounded. She had been stabbed once with a sword.

But why?

Hool Haji looked up at me as I stood on the other side of the prone girl. "It is too much," he said in a hollow voice. "First that—and now this."

"Is it Priosa work?" I asked quietly.

He nodded, checking her pulse. "She is dying," he said. "It is a wonder she has lived so long with that wound."

As if in response to his voice, Ora Lis' eyes fluttered open. They were glazed but brightened in recognition when they saw Hool Haji.

A choking sob escaped the girl's throat and she spoke with difficulty, almost in a whisper.

"Oh, my Bradhi!"

Hool Haji stroked her arm, trying to frame words which would not come. Plainly he blamed himself for this tragedy.

"My Bradhi—I am sorry."

"Sorry!" Words came now. "It is not you, Ora Lis, who should feel sorry—it is I."

"No!" Her voice gained strength. "You do not realize what I have done. Is there time?"

"Time? Time for what?" Hool Haji was puzzled, though some sort of realization was beginning to dawn in my mind.

"Time to stop the Priosa."

"From what?"

Ora Lis coughed weakly and blood flecked her lips.

"I—I told them where you were..."

She tried to rise then. "I told them where you were… Do you not understand? I told them of the meeting! I was mad. It—it was my grief. Oh…"

Hool Haji looked at me again, his eyes full of misery. He realized now. It had been Ora Lis who had betrayed us—her revenge on Hool Haji for his rejection of her.

Then he looked down at her. What he said to her then told me once and for all that he was a man in every sense—a man of strength and of pity also.

"No," he said, "they have done nothing. We will warn the— village—at once."

She died saying nothing more. There was a smile of relief on her lips.

We buried the ill-starred girl in the loamy soil of the hills. We did not mark her grave. Something in us seemed to tell us not to—that in buying Ora Lis in an unmarked grave it was as if we sought to bury the whole tragic episode.

It was impossible, of course.

Later that day we were joined by several more fleeing Mendishar. We learned that the Priosa were hunting down all survivors, that they were hot on the heels of the warriors who had escaped. We also learned that a few prisoners had been taken, though the survivors could not name them, and that the village had been razed.

One of the town-leaders, a warrior in middle age called Khal Hira, said as we rode, "I would still like to discover who betrayed us. I have racked my brains and can think of no explanation."

I glanced at Hool Haji and he looked at me. It was at that moment, perhaps—though it might have been earlier—that we entered into an unspoken agreement to say nothing of Ora Lis. Let it remain a mystery. The only true villains were the Priosa. The rest were victims of fate.

We did not answer Khal Hira at all. We did not speak thereafter.

None of us was in any mood for conversation.

The hills gave way to plains and the plains to desert country as we fled in defeat from the Priosa pursuers.

They did not catch us—but they drove some of us, indirectly, to our deaths.

CHAPTER FIVE
The Tower in the Desert

KHAL HIRA'S LIPS were swollen but firmly clenched as he stared out over the desert.

Desert it was—no longer a bare wasteland of cracked earth and rock, but a place of black sand stirred into constantly shifting life by a perpetual breeze.

We no longer found pools of brackish water, no longer knew, even roughly, where we were, save that we had travelled north-west.

Our tough mounts were almost as weary as we were and beginning to flag. Here the sky was cloudless and the sun a throbbing, burning enemy.

For five days we had ridden the desert, rather aimlessly. Our minds were still stunned by the sudden turn of events at the village. We were still badly demoralized, and unless we were able to find water soon we should die. Our bodies were grimed with the thick black desert sand and we were slumped in our saddles with weariness.

There was nothing for it but to keep moving, to continue our hopeless quest for water.

It was on the sixth day that Khal Hira keeled from his saddle. He uttered no sound and when we went to his assistance we discovered he was dead.

Two more died on the following day. Apart from Hool Haji and myself, three others remained alive—if "alive" is the proper word to use. These were Jil Deera, Vas Oola and Bac Puri. The first was a stocky warrior of even fewer words than his fellows and very short for a Mendishar. The other two were tall young men. Of the pair, Bac Puri was beginning to show visible signs of losing his grip. I could not blame him—very soon the beating sun would drive us all mad, even if it did not kill us first.

Bac Puri was beginning to mutter to himself and his eyes were rolling dreadfully. We pretended not to notice, partly for his sake, partly for our own. His condition seemed prophetic of the state we ourselves would soon be reaching.

Then we saw the tower.

I had seen nothing like it on Mars. Though partially ruined and seeming incredibly ancient, it bore no trace of erosion. Its partial destruction seemed to be the result of some bombardment, its upper sections having great jagged holes blown through them at some stage in the tower's history.

It offered shelter, if nothing else. But it also told us that once there had been a settlement here—and where there had been a settlement there might have been water.

Reaching the tower and touching it, I was astounded to discover that it was of no natural substance—at least none that I could recognize. It seemed to be made of some immmensely durable plastic as strong as steel—stronger, perhaps, since it had withstood any sort of damage from the corrosive sand.

We entered, my companions being forced to duck. Sand had drifted into the tower, but it was cool. We collapsed to the ground and, no one having spoken, almost immediately fell asleep.

I was the first to awake. This was probably because I had not yet become fully used to the longer Martian night.

It was barely dawn and I still felt weak though refreshed.

Even in the condition I was in I felt curiosity about the tower. There was a roof about twelve feet above my head, but no apparent means of reaching the upper floor, which must obviously be there.

Leaving my sleeping companions, I began to explore the surrounding desert, looking for some sign of water lying somewhere beneath the sand.

I was sure that it must, but whether I would find it was an entirely different matter.

Then my eyes caught sight of a projection in the sand. It was not a dune. Inspecting it, I found it to be a kind of low wall made of the same material as the tower. However, when I scraped away the sand I saw that the wall enclosed a surface also of the same material. I could not make out the purpose of this construction.

It was laid out in a perfect square some thirty feet across. I began to walk towards the opposite wall.

I was not cautious enough—or perhaps I was too weary—for I suddenly put one foot upon yielding sand, tried to recover as I lost my balance, failed and fell downwards through the surface. I landed, winded and bruised, in a chamber half filled with sand. Rolling over and looking up, I saw that there was a jagged hole above me through which daylight filtered. The hole seemed to have been caused by the same thing that had torn the holes in the tower. Some attempt had been made to patch it and it was across the makeshift patch that sand had blown. It was through this that I had fallen.

The patch was flimsy, originally a sheet of light plastic. I looked at a piece that had fallen with me. Again I could not recognize the substance, although not being a chemist I could not say whether the process was familiar on Earth of my own time or not. Like the tower, however, it spoke of an advanced technology not possessed by any of the Martian races with whom I had come in contact.

Suddenly my weariness seemed to fall away from me as a thought struck me. The thought had many implications but I confess I did not think of my companions above but of myself.

Was this a dwelling of the Sheev? If so, there might be a chance of being able to return to that Mars of the age I needed to visit—the age in which my Shizala lived!

I spat the harsh sand from my mouth and stood up. The chamber was almost featureless, though, as my eyes grew accustomed to the gloom, I made out a small panel on the far wall. Inspecting this I saw it consisted of half-a-dozen small studs. My hand hovered over them. If I pressed one, what would happen? Would anything happen? Maybe it was unlikely—yet the hand which had patched the roof might have kept any machinery alive. Was the place occupied? I was sure that other chambers opened off from this one. It was logical. If there were control studs there was machinery.

I pressed a stud at random. The result was rather anticlimactic, for all that happened was that dim light filled the chamber, issuing from the walls themselves. This light revealed something else—a rectangular hairline close to the panel, speaking of a door. I had been right.

And the power—or some of it, at any rate—was still working.

Before exploring further I cautioned myself and returned to my position immediately below the gap in the roof. I heard faint voices. Evidently my companions had awakened, wondered where I was and had come to find me.

I called upwards.

Soon I saw Hool Haji's face staring down at me in surprise.

"What have you found, Michael Kane?"

"Perhaps our salvation," I said with a passable imitation of a grin. "Come down—bring the others—see for yourselves what I've discovered."

Soon Hool Haji dropped down into the chamber, followed by Jil Deera and Vas Oola. Bac Puri was the last to swing downwards, looking intensely suspicious and still half mad.

"Water?" said Bac Puri. "Have you found water?"

I shook my head. "No. But perhaps we shall."

"Perhaps! Perhaps! I am dying!"

Hool Haji put a hand on Bac Puri's shoulder. "Calm yourself, friend. Have patience."

Bac Puri's tongue moved slowly across his swollen lips and he sank into a mood of sullen gloom. Only his eyes continued to dart about.

"What are these?" Jil Deera waved his hand towards the studs.

"One of them brought this light," I said. "I presume that another activates the door—I cannot guess which."

"And what lies beyond the door? I wonder," put in Vas Oola.

I shook my head. Then I reached out and pressed another stud. The chamber began to vibrate slightly. Hastily I pressed the stud again and the vibration ceased. Pressing a third stud brought no apparent result.

A fourth produced a shrill, whining sound and a grating noise which, I quickly saw, indicated that the door was opening, sliding into the right-hand wall.

At first, peering into the aperture revealed, we saw nothing but pitch darkness and felt cold, cold air on our faces.

"Who do you think created this place?" I whispered to Hool Haji. "The Sheev?"

"It could have been the Sheev, yes." He did not seem very certain.

I reached my hand inside and felt about for a panel that should, logically, correspond with the one in the chamber in which we stood.

I found it. I pressed the corresponding stud and light filled the other chamber.

There was no sand in this one. It was roughly the same shape as the one we were in but there were large, spherical objects set into the walls on one side. Beneath them were what were plainly controls of some kind.

Lying on the floor was a skeleton.

Seeing the remains of what had evidently been a blue giant of the Mendishar, Bac Puri let out a shriek and pointed a shaking finger at the bones.

"An omen! He, too, was curious. He was slain. There is some supernatural agency at work here!"

Affecting insouciance, I stepped into the chamber and bent towards the skeleton.

"Nonsense," I said, stooping and wrenching a short-shafted spear from the remains. "He was slain by this—look!" I held up the lance. It was light and strong, made all in one piece, again of advanced materials.

"I have seen nothing like that in my life," Jil Deera said, joining me and looking curiously at the weapon. "And see—these symbols engraved on the shaft—they are in no language I recognize."

I also did not recognize the language as the basic common tongue of Mars. There were still similarities—though much fainter—to ancient Sanskrit, however. The essential form of the script was the same.

"What is it, do you know?" I said, passing the spear to Hool Haji.

He pursed his lips. "I have seen something like it in my wanderings. It is like that of the Sheev, but not quite." His hand was not completely steady as he handed the spear back to me.

"Then what is it?" I asked, somewhat impatiently.

"It is—"

Then there came a chilling sound. It was high and preternatural—a kind of whisper which echoed through the chambers. It came from beyond the chamber in which we stood—from deep within the underground complex.

It was one of the vilest sounds I have heard in my life. It seemed to confirm Bac Puri's half-insane speculation of some supernatural residents of the place. Suddenly, from being a refuge, the underground chamber became a place full of fear—and a terror which was hard to control.

My first impulse was to flee—and, indeed, Bac Puri was already inching towards the door through which we'd come. The others were less decisive but evidently they shared my feelings.

I laughed—or attempted to, the result being a kind of mirthless croak—and said: "Come now—this is an ancient place. The sound could be made by some animal that inhabits the ruins; it could have its cause in machinery, or even the wind passing through the chambers…"

I did not believe a word I said and neither did they.

I changed my approach. "Well," I said with a shrug, "what shall we do? Risk a danger that may be no danger at all, or go to certain death in the desert? It will be a slow death."

Bac Puri paused. Some remnant of his earlier strength of character must have come to his assistance. He squared his shoulders and rejoined us.

I strode past the skeleton and pressed the stud to open the next door.

The door opened smoothly this time and I quickly found the next stud to illuminate the third chamber. This one was bigger.

In a sense it comforted me, for it was full of machinery. Of course, I did not recognize the function of the machines, but the thought that some high intelligence must have created them was comforting in itself. As a scientist, I could appreciate the workmanship alone. This was the work of ordinary, intelligent men—it had not been created by any supernatural being.

If inhabitants still lived in this honeycomb of chambers then they would be folk to whom logic would appeal. Perhaps they would bear us some animosity, perhaps they would possess superior weapons—but at least they would be a tangible foe.

So I thought.

I should have realized that there was a flaw in the argument which I so rationally gave to myself to quiet my feelings of disturbance.

I should have realized that the sound I had heard was animal in origin and malevolent in content. There had been no spark of true intelligence in it.

We moved on, chamber by chamber, discovering more machines and great lockers of materials; cloth not unlike parachute silk; containers of gas and chemicals; strong reels of cord similar to nylon cord but even stronger; laboratory equipment used in experiments with chemicals, electronics and the like; parts of machines, things that were obviously power units of some kind.

The further in to the great complex of chambers we moved, the less ordered were the things we found. They were neatly stacked and positioned in the earlier chambers, but in the later ones containers had been overturned, lockers opened and their contents strewn about. Had the place been visited by looters, represented by the dead man in the second chamber?

I don't know which chamber it was—perhaps the thirtieth—which I opened in the usual way. I reached in my hand to pres the light stud—and felt something soft and damp touch my skin. It was a horrible touch. With a gasp I withdrew my hand and turned to tell my companions of what had happened.

The first thing I saw was Bac Puri's face, eyes wide and full of terror.

He was pointing into the chamber. A strangled sound escaped his throat. He dropped his hand and fumbled for his sword.

The others' hands also went to their swords.

I turned back—and saw them.

White shapes.

Perhaps they had once been human.

They were human no longer.

With a feeling of mingled horror and desperation, I too drew my sword, feeling that no ordinary weapon could possibly defend me against the apparitions that moved towards us out of the darkness.

CHAPTER SIX

The Once-Were-Men

BAC PURI DID not flee this time.

His face worked in a peculiar contortion. He took half a step backwards and then, before we could stop him, flung himself into the darkened chamber, straight at the corpse-white creatures!

They gibbered and fell back for a moment, a terrible twittering noise, like that of thousands of bats, filling the air and echoing on and on through the complex of chambers.

Bac Puri's sword swung to left and right, up and down, slicing off limbs, stabbing vitals, piercing the unnaturally soft, clammy bodies.

And then he was, as if by magic, a mass of spears. He howled in his pain and madness as javelins like the one we had seen earlier appeared in every part of his body until it was almost impossible to distinguish the man beneath.

He fell with a crash.

Seeing the creatures were at least mortal, I decided we should take advantage of Bac Puri's mad attack and, waving my sword, I leapt through the entrance, shouting:

"Come—they can be slain!"

They could be slain, but they were elusive creatures and sight and feel of them brought physical revulsion. With the others behind me, I carried the attack to them and soon found myself in a tangle of soft, yielding flesh that seemed boneless.

And the faces! They were vile parodies of human faces and again resembled nothing quite so much as the ugly little vampire bat of Earth. Flat faces with huge nostrils let into the head, gashes of mouths full of sharp little fangs, half-blind eyes, dark and wicked—and insensate.

As I fought their claws, their sharp teeth and their spears, they slithered about, gibbering and twittering.

I had been wrong about them. There was not a trace of intelligence in their faces—just a demoniac blood-hunger, a dark malevolence that hated, hated, hated—but never reasoned.

My companions and I stood shoulder to shoulder, back to back, as the things tore at us.

When we saw that our heavy swords could affect them—and had in fact already dispatched dozens of them—our spirits rose.

At length the ghouls turned and fled, leaving only the wounded flopping on the floor. We slew these. There was nothing else we could do.

We attempted to follow them through the far door, but it closed swiftly and, when we opened it, the creatures had passed on through the complex.

The light stud worked and showed us the dead creatures better.

Bac Puri, in his madness, had undoubtedly helped save our lives. In attacking the creatures he had taken most of their javelins into his body.

These inhabitants of the underground complex were slightly smaller than me and seemed, though this was incredible, to possess hardly any skeleton at all. Our weapons had sliced through flesh and muscle, had drawn blood—if the thin yellow stuff that stained our blades could be called blood—but had met no resistance from bone.

Steeling myself to inspect the corpses closer, I saw that there was a skeleton of sorts but the bones were so thin and brittle that they resembled fine, ivory wires.

What strange, aberrant branch of the evolutionary tree did these creatures spring from?

I turned to Hool Haji.

"What race is this?" I asked. "I think you had guessed earlier."

"Not the Sheev," he said with a faint, ironic grimace. "Nor the Yaksha, either—and I suspected that it was the Yaksha before I saw them. These pitiful things are no real threat, unless it be to the mind!"

"So you thought they were a race called the Yaksha—why?"

"Because the language on their spears and on their instruments and cabinets is the written language of the Yaksha."

"Who are the Yaksha? I seem to remember you mentioning them."

"Are? Perhaps *were* is a better word, for they still exist only in rumour and superstitious speculation. They are cousins of the Sheev. Do you not remember me telling you about them when we first met?"

Now it came back! Of course—the elder race who had seduced the Argzoon away from Mendishar in the first place, during the war the Martians called the Mightiest War.

"I think these must be descendants of the Yaksha, however," Hool Haji continued, "for they bear slight similarities to that race, if I was told aright. They have probably existed down here for countless centuries, somehow remembering—in ritual form, doubtless—to keep the machinery running and defend the place against outsiders. Bit by bit they lost all intelligence and—you will notice—seem to prefer darkness to light, although light is available to them. It is a fitting fate for the remnants of an evil race."

I shuddered. I could sympathize in my own way with the creatures that had once been men.

Then another thought struck me.

"Well," I said, somewhat more cheerfully, "whatever they are biologically, they must have need of water. That means that somewhere here we shall soon find what we need."

Our need seemed to have diminished with the finding of the underground chambers, but the fight had weakened us further and water was our prime necessity.

Warily, but with more confidence that we could meet and defeat any of the white creatures that attacked us, we moved on until we entered a chamber larger than the rest through which a little *natural* light filtered!

Looking up I saw that the light seemed to come through a domed roof, much higher then the roofs of most of the chambers we had passed through. Sand had filtered in through some cracks in this roof, but the floor was not deep in the stuff.

And then I heard it!

A tinkling sound, a splashing sound. A first I thought that thirst had driven me mad but then, as my eyes grew better accustomed to the gloom, I saw it—a fountain in the center of the chamber. A large pool of cool water!

We moved forward and tasted the stuff cautiously before drinking. It was pure and fresh.

We drank sparingly, wetting our bodies all over whilst we took turns to stand guard against any possible attack from the local residents!

Refreshed and in good spirits, we filled our belt canteens. The stopper of mine was stuck, clogged by the dust. I took the little skinning knife from the right-hand side of my harness—a knife which every blue Martians carries. It is half hidden in the decoration of the leather so that, if captured by an enemy, that enemy might overlook the knife and give the captured warrior a chance to escape. I worked the stopper loose, then returned the knife to its hidden sheath in my harness.

What now?

We had not inclination to explore the remaining chambers. We had seen enough for the moment. We took the precaution, however, of going to the far door through which the white things had doubtless fled, and blocked it as best we could with sand and loose masonry.

I next discovered a ladder consisting of rungs let into the wall and leading up towards the roof where a narrow gallery ran around the chamber, at the point where the dome began. I climbed this ladder and climbed on to the gallery. It was just large enough to take me and had evidently been intended simply for the use of workmen either repairing or decorating the dome.

The dome was not made of the same durable synthetic material as the rest of the place. I put my eye to a crack and looked out over a seemingly endless expanse of black desert, shining now, like crystal, in the sun. The dome seemed half buried and was probably all but invisible from outside.

A piece of the material came away in my hand. It was in an advanced stage of corrosion and would soon collapse altogether. It was transparent—evidently designed to admit light into the chamber of the fountain. Probably the place had been the central hall for relaxing when the Yaksha had been sane and human. The dome had not been planned for any purely functional purpose so much as for decoration. This must be why it would soon collapse. When it did the sand would come in, the fountain would be blocked, and I did not think the inhabitants of the underground city would have the intelligence to clear the sand away—or, for that matter, repair the dome.

Repairs had been made earlier in the roof, but I guessed by more intelligent ancestors of the present dwellers.

I returned to the ground, an idea slowly taking shape in my mind.

At its base the dome was some thirty feet across—ample space for a large object to pass through.

"Why are you looking so thoughtful, my friend?" asked Hool Haji.

"I think I know a way of escape," I said.

"From this space? We need only retrace our steps."

"Or break through the roof, for that matter," I said, pointing upwards. "It is very flimsy—eroded from the outside by the sand. But I meant escape from our main predicament—escape from the desert."

"Have you found a map somewhere?"

"No, but I have found many other things. All the artifacts of a great scientific culture—strong, airtight fabric, cord—gas containers. I hope they still contain gas and that it is the kind I need."

Hool Haji was completely mystified.

I smiled. The others were now looking at me as if I had followed Bac Puri's example and was losing control of my mind.

"It was the dome gave me the idea, for some reason," I said. "It struck me that if we had a—a flying ship we could cross the desert in no time."

"A flying ship! I have heard of such things—some Southern races still possess a few, I believe." It was Jil Deera who spoke now. "Have you found one?"

"No." I shook my head, still thinking deeply.

"Then why speak of such a thing?" Vas Oola spoke somewhat sharply.

"Because I think we could *make* one," I said.

"Make one?" Hool Haji smiled. "We have not the knowledge of the old races. It would be impossible."

"I have some little technical knowledge," I said, "though not as much as was once possessed, evidently, by this vanished race. I had not thought of building an aircraft of so advanced a kind as theirs."

"Then what?"

"A primitive aircraft could be built, I think." The three blue men regarded me in silence—still a trifle suspicious.

There was no word for the kind of aircraft I had in mind—no Martian word. I used the English derivation from the French.

"It would be called a *balloon*," I said.

I began to sketch in the sand, explaining the principle of the balloon.

"We should have to make a gas-bag from the material we found back there," I said. "There will be difficulties, of course—the bag must be airtight for a start. From it we suspend ropes attached to a cabin—that will be the thing in which we ride…"

By the time I had finished talking and sketching, the intelligent men of Mendishar believed me and largely understood me— which was remarkable considering they came from a society which was mainly non-technical. Once again I had experienced the robust open-mindedness of the Martian who, on the whole, can be taught any concept in a very short time if it is explained to him in sufficiently logical terms. They were an old race of course, and had the example of the earlier, highly-civilized races—the

Sheev and the Yaksha—to show them that what often seemed impossible need not necessarily be.

Enthusiastically, we returned through the underground chambers selecting the things we needed.

I was not at all sure that the *right* gas would be found in the banks of containers that occupied several of the rooms. I took my life in my hands and began to sniff a little of each gas. The containers had valves which still worked perfectly.

Some of the gases were unfamiliar, but none seemed particularly poisonous, though one or two made me a trifle dizzy for a short time.

At last I found the set of containers I needed. They contained a gas with the atomic number 2, the symbol *He*, atomic weight 4.0026, a gas which took its name from the Greek word for the sun—Helium. Non-inflammable and very light, it was what I had been seeking—the perfect gas for filling my balloon!

The search became intensive after I had ascertained that the basic things we needed were there—the light fabric, the gas, the ropes. Next I began to inspect the motors we had found. I did not take them to pieces since I guessed they had some kind of nuclear base—that the power came from a tiny atomic engine. But I did find out how they operated and saw that they would be very simple to harness to propellers.

There were no propellers, however—nothing that would serve as propellers. These would have to be made, somehow.

Our next great discovery was of a machine that could be keyed to turn out sections of the tough, light synthetic material of which so much of the place was built.

The machine was large and evidently connected to some unseen reservoir.

It was a boon to us. On a panel in front one made a careful drawing of the part wanted. This had to be done like a plan—side-view, top-view and front-view. The size of the required piece was selected, buttons were pressed and, within minutes, the part came out into a pan lying beneath the main machine.

We could have as many propellers as we needed—indeed, we could have our cabin custom-built, too. I wished then that I might have more time to saunter around this fantastic underground city and discover just what powered it, what synthesis of elements produced the super-strong plastic, how the machine worked... I resolved to return as soon as I could, bring with me men who could be trained to work with me on a project that would have as its ultimate end of the wrestling of all the city's secrets from it, the correlation of information, the analysis of machines and materials.

When that came about, a new age would dawn on Mars!

Meanwhile we worked hard, transporting all the things we needed into the domed hall where, apart from anything else, we were close to the water supply.

We also found dehydrated food in air-tight containers. This food was tasteless but nourishing.

As the balloon began to take shape our spirits rose higher and higher.

During this time we did not forget to look after our personal appearance. I made a point of shaving regularly—although the only mirror I could find was a great reflector as big as me which I somehow dragged into the domed chamber simply to use as a shaving mirror!

While Jil Deera and Vas Oola worked on the balloon—we had found that the pressure of a warm human hand on the fabric served to weld it together, facilitating the making of the gas-bag—Hool Haji and I climbed the wall and began to finish nature's work of breaking open the dome.

In order that the inhabitants of the place might continue to live—if life it was—we had constructed a kind of hatch-cover which could be fitted in place of the dome to stop sand drifting down and clogging the fountain.

Soon the helium tanks were fitted to the valve of the gas-bag and the four of us watched the great mound of fabric slowly fill out.

We had not yet fitted the driving bands to engine and propeller shaft, but apart from that the balloon was ready. It was in all essential respects a powered airship and, though slower and more vulnerable than the Martian aircraft that I had encountered, would do its job well, I thought.

Soon the gas-bag was taut. The balloon began to strain at its mooring ropes and looked as if it could lift a hundred such as us. We began to laugh and slap one another on the back—though it was a bit of a stretch for me to slap Hool Haji's back! We had done it!

The cabin was enclosed, suspended from the strong ropes that covered the outside of the gas-bag. It was made of sections of synthetic material and had open port-holes. Unfortunately we had found no means of providing transparent panes, so we had to construct shutters instead. Inside it was provisioned with water, spare gas tanks and dehydrated food.

We were very proud of the ship. Crude it may have been, but it was soundly constructed and soon, when we had let her up through the roof a bit and fitted the driving bands to the engine, we should be ready to go wherever we chose. Probably back to Mendishar where, as Hool Haji pointed out, the arrival of their leader, thought dead or chased away from the country, in a flying ship would probably hearten the populace to such an extent that much that had been lost in the attack on the village might be regained by this spectacular return!

Hool Haji and the other two blue giants were talking earnestly about this possibility when the opposite door—the one we had blocked against any attempt of the white ghouls to enter—began to melt.

The material which I had regarded as indestructible was bubbling and running like cheap plastic in a fire. A terrible smell—acrid and sweet at the same time—began to come from the door.

I did not know what was happening but I acted nonetheless.

"Quick," I yelled. "Into the balloon!"

I pushed at my companions, helping them clamber into the cabin.

Then I turned as the door collapsed completely—and there were several of the white inhabitants of the place.

In their hands was a machine.

Plainly they did not know what it was. All they knew was enough to hold it and point it.

It was an odd paradox—a machine so advanced as that in the hands of those imbeciles.

It was emitting a ray—a ray which struck the opposite wall now, narrowly missing the balloon and me. A heat ray, doubtless. A laser ray!

It was then that I realized no one had cut the mooring lines.

I sprang towards them, drawing my sword.

I knew, in fact, that the knowledge of portable lasers had belonged to the older race. I should have been prepared for something like this.

In their insensate rage these descendants of the Yaksha had perhaps dredged up some race memory, found the projector and brought it back to deal out death to the interlopers.

Whatever the cause, we should all be dead soon unless I was swift. I sliced the mooring ropes.

Hool Haji yelled at me from the cabin as he saw what I was doing.

The balloon began to rise, gently bumping the roof. Shortly the gas would take them to safety as it sought the air beyond the roof. The aperture created by breaking the dome was just wide enough to take it.

Now the ghouls leveled the laser at me again. I was bound to be killed by it. The ray was sweeping the room, melting or slicing apart everything it touched.

And then the idea came!

CHAPTER SEVEN
City of the Spiders

As THE BEAM came closer and closer, weaving somewhat at random in the hands of the moronic ghouls, I suddenly saw the great reflector which I had been using as a shaving mirror.

It was a powerful reflector. It might work.

Quickly I rushed towards it and got behind it.

The laser beam sliced away part of the fountain which fell with a splash into the water. The fountain spurted sporadically now.

The beam came closer and melted a whole section of the wall, revealing the next chamber beyond. The white things shuffled closer, their soft, near-boneless arms cradling the powerful projector.

Then the beam struck the reflector.

Laser-rays are concentrated light. A mirror reflects light. A powerful mirror might reflect powerful light rays.

This one did.

The mirror bent the ray and spread it for a few moments. Then for a few seconds it turned the whole ray back on those who were directing it.

Most of the white ghouls were shriveled in a second. The rest yelled in terror, retreated a short way and then came at me yelling!

I dashed for one of the dangling mooring lines just as the balloon began to ascend through the aperture.

I grabbed the last few feet of the line.

As claws scraped at me I began to haul myself up towards the cabin.

Then the balloon was shooting into the air and, in that moment of escaping the danger of the white creatures and finding myself in a new danger, I realized that we had forgotten one vital thing in our haste to escape.

We had forgotten to load our ballast—the balloon was rising too rapidly!

Twice I was nearly shaken from my hand-hold as I clung desperately to the rope, trying to pull myself towards the cabin.

Then I saw Hool Haji open the hatch of the cabin and, balancing with only a toe-hold on the outside of the cabin, he stretched out and grabbed the rope from which I was suspended.

The ground was far below, the black, shining desert spinning beneath me.

Hool Haji managed to drag himself back into the cabin, still clutching the rope. Then he and the other two began to haul me in.

My hands were aching and torn by the friction. I was almost ready to let go.

Just as I felt I could hang on no longer I felt their great hands seize me and drag me in to the cabin. They closed the hatch.

Panting with exhaustion and relief, I lay on the floor of the cabin until I had recovered my breath. We were still rising far too rapidly and would soon escape the slightly thinner Martian atmosphere—it must be remembered that the atmosphere of that age was much thicker than it is now.

I rose shakily and went to the controls. They were simple, makeshift controls and would have been tested before we took the air if we had had the chance. Now we would have to see if they worked. If they did not, we were done for.

I pulled a lever which controlled the valve of the gas-bag. I had to let gas out and hope that it would be just enough and not so much that it would send us plummeting earthwards!

Slowly our altitude leveled out and I knew the control was working.

But we were still drifting at random on the air-currents. We would have to land and fix the driving bands to the engine. Under power we should be able to return to Mendishar in less than a day.

I was rather annoyed at this waste of our valuable helium, but there was nothing else for it. Very slowly, I began to take the ship down.

We were still some two thousand feet up when it seemed the balloon was suddenly kicked by an enormous foot and buffeted about, sending us all flying. I could not keep my footing and was hurled away from the control panel.

I believe I lost consciousness for some time.

When I came to my senses it was almost dark. There was now no longer the sensation of being the ball in some game played by giants far more huge than my blue companions but a sense, instead, of speeding along at tremendous velocity.

I rose unsteadily and went to a port-hole, sliding back a shutter.

I looked down and at first could not believe what I saw.

We were heading over the sea—a rough, storm-tossed sea. We were traveling at a good hundred miles an hour—probably more.

But what was propelling us?

It was a natural force of some kind. It seemed to be a wind by the moaning and howling sound that reached my ears.

But what kind of wind could have struck so rapidly without warning?

I turned back to find that Hool Haji was beginning to stir. He, too, had been knocked out.

I helped him up and together we revived our companions.

"What is it, Hool Haji? Do you know?" I asked.

He rubbed his face with his big hand. "I should have watched the calendar more carefully," he said.

"Why?"

"I did not mention this because I felt that we should either be out of the desert or dead—that was before we found the tower and the underground city. I did not mention it while we were underground because I knew we should be safe, there being no sign of damage to the city."

"What didn't you mention? What?"

"I am sorry—it is my fault. Probably the reason why the city of the Yaksha has not been reported is because of the Roaring Death."

"What is the Roaring Death?"

"A great wind that periodically crosses the desert. Some think that it was originally the *cause* of the desert, that before the Roaring Death came the desert existed as a fertile place. Perhaps the city of the Yaksha was built before the coming of the Roaring Death. I do not know—but the Roaring Death has crossed the desert for centuries, producing mighty sandstorms, leveling everything."

"And where does the wind go?" I asked. "For we might as well know since we're being borne along by it."

"Westwards," said Hool Haji.

"Over the sea?"

"Just so."

"And where then?"

"I do not know."

I went to the port-hole again and looked down.

The troubled sea, cold and dark, still lay below us, but through the gloom I thought I could make out, very faintly, some sort of land-mass.

"What lies beyond the western sea?" I asked Hool Haji.

"I do not know—a land unexplored, save along its coasts. An evil land by all accounts."

The land was almost below us now.

"Evil? What makes you say that?" I asked my friend.

"Legends—travellers' tales—exploration parties that never return. The Western Continent is a place of jungles and strange beasts. It was the continent worst struck by the struggles of the Mightiest War. When the war was over, so they say, strange changes took place in nature—men, animals, plants were all—altered—by something that was left behind after the Mightiest War. Some say this was a spirit, some say a kind of gas, others a machine. But, whatever the reason, the continent in the West has always been avoided by sane men."

"All that seems to indicate is an atomic war, radiation and mutation," I mused. "And in the thousands of years since the war took place it is unlikely that there is any dangerous radiation. We need not fear from that."

Some of the words I used were in English since, though there probably were words to describe the things of which I spoke, they were not in the current Martian vocabulary.

The "Roaring Death" was beginning to abate, it seemed, for our movement became slower.

I felt that our fate was out of my hands as we sped deeper inland.

The two moons of Mars dashed through the sky above us, illuminating the sight of strange, waving jungles of peculiar colourings.

I must admit that the peculiar vegetation did disturb me somewhat, but I told myself that we could come to no harm while we rode the wind at this altitude.

When the wind no longer bore us along we could land at leisure, fix the engines and, under power, go where we wished.

The opportunity did not come for some hours. Where the wind came from and where it finally died I could not tell—unless it circled the globe permanently, gathering force as it travelled. I was no meteorologist.

At last we were able to escape the airstream and drift towards the huge trees whose dense foliage seemed to form a solid mass below us.

Great, shiny leaves waved on sinuous boughs and the colours were shades of black, brown, dark green and mottled red.

A sense of evil hung heavily on this jungle and we did not like the prospect of having to land in it. But at length, by morning, we found a clearing large enough to take the balloon and we began to descend.

We landed quite neatly for such unskilled aeronauts. We moored the ship and inspected it for damage. The Yaksha building materials had stood up to a wind that would have shaken almost anything else to pieces. There was comparatively little damage, considering the buffeting we had taken.

All we had to do now was spend an hour or so fixing the driving bands and finding something that would serve as ballast. Then we'd top up the helium—and be heading for Mendishar in no time.

We soon had the engines working well and the propellers spinning.

While we worked, however, we began to get a definite sense of being watched. We saw nothing save the dark jungle, its trees rising several hundred feet into the air and all tangled together to form a lattice of twisting boles going up and up on all sides, covered in a tangle of other vegetation—warm and damp-smelling.

How the glade could ever have been formed I do not know. It was a freak of nature. Its floor consisted of nothing but smooth, hard mud almost the consistency of rock. At its edge grew the dark, shiny leaves of the lower shrubs, a tangle of vines that, from the corner of one's eye, tended to look like fat snakes, unhealthy-looking bushes and creepers gathered around the spreading roots of the trees.

I had never seen anything so big in a forest. There seemed to be a variety of levels stretching up and up so that from the outside the forest looked like a gigantic cliff in which were dark openings of caves.

It was easy for one to imagine being watched. I suspected that it was only my imagination at work, for the surroundings were such that they set the subconscious going nineteen to the dozen!

Now all we had to do was find ballast. Jil Deera suggested that logs cut from the branches of trees might do as well as anything. It would be a crude ballast but would probably serve us adequately.

While Jil Deera and Vas Oola aided me in putting the finishing touches to the motor, Hool Haji said he would go and get some logs.

Off he went. We finished our work and waited for him to return. We were impatient to get out of this mysterious jungle and return to Mendishar as soon as possible.

By late afternoon we had shouted ourselves hoarse but Hool Haji had not replied to us.

There was nothing for it but to enter the forest and see if he was hurt—possibly knocked unconscious in some minor accident.

Vas Oola and Jil Deera said they would search with me, but I told them our balloon was all-important—they must stay with it and guard it. I managed to convince them of this.

I found the spot where Hool Haji had entered the forest and began to follow his trail.

It was not difficult. Being a large man, he had left many signs of his passing. In some places he had hacked away some of the undergrowth.

The forest was dark and dank. My feet trod on yielding, rotting plants and sometimes sank to the mire beneath. I continued calling my friend's name, but he still did not reply.

And then I came upon traces of a fight and knew that I had not imagined we were being watched after all!

Here I found Hool Haji's sword. He would never have discarded that unless captured—or killed!

I scouted around for signs of captors but could find none!

This was very perplexing, for I rather prided myself on my tracking ability. All I could notice were signs of some sticky substance, like strands of fine silk, adhering to the surrounding foliage.

Later on I discovered some more of this stuff and decided that, since it was my only clue, I would look for more in the hope that Hool Haji's captors—or murderers—had left it behind them, thought why they should and what it was I had no idea.

I hardly realized, as night was falling, that I had come to a city.

The city seemed to be one large building sprawling through the jungle. It appeared to grow out of the jungle, merge with it, be part of it. It was of dark, ancient obsidian and, in crevices, earth and seeds had fallen so that small trees and shrubs grew out of the city. There were ziggurats and domes all appearing to flow together in the half light. It was easy to believe that this was some strange freak of nature, that rock had simply flowed and solidified into the *appearance* of a city!

Yet here and there were windows, entrances, all obscured by plants.

As night fell the city glowed very, very dimly, catching the few faint moonbeams that were able to penetrate the forest roof so far above.

This must be where my friend's enemies had brought him. It was a daunting place.

Wearily I entered the city, climbing over the heaped, glassy rock, searching for some sign of the inhabitants, some indication as to where my friend was hidden.

I clambered up the sloping sides of buildings, over roofs, down walls, searching, searching. Everywhere were deep shadows and the feel of smooth, lumpy rock beneath my hands and feet.

There were no streets in this city, simply depressions in the roof which covered it. I entered one of these gullies—a deep one—and began to inch along it, feeling desperate.

Something scuttled up the wall to my left and I felt sick as I saw what it was—the largest spider I had ever seen in my life.

Now I saw others. I took a firm grip on Hool Haji's sword and prepared to draw my own as well. The spiders were as big as footballs!

I was just preparing to leave the gully and ascend another sloping wall of green rock when suddenly I felt something drop over my head and shoulders. I tried to strike it away with the sword but it clung to me. The more I moved the more entangled I became.

Now I understood why there had been no corpses at the scene of Hool Haji's capture!

The thing that had fallen on me was a net of the same fine, sticky silk I had seen in the forest. It was strong and clung to everything it touched.

Now I had fallen face downwards and was still trying to disentangle myself.

I felt bony hands pick me up.

I looked at those who had trapped me. I could not believe my eyes. To the waist they were men, though considerably shorter than me, with wiry bodies bulging with lumpy muscles. They had large eyes and slit mouths, but were still recognizable as human beings—until you looked beyond their waists and at the eight furry legs that radiated from them. The bodies of men and the legs of spiders!

I now made jabbing movements at the leader—my arms were so restricted it was all I could manage.

The leader was expressionless as he pointed a long pole at me. The end of this pole seemed to be fitted with a needle-like tip some six inches long. He struck this into me—but only a short way. I tried to fight back and then, almost at once, felt my whole body go rigid.

I could not move a muscle. I could not even blink. I had been injected with a poison, that was plain—a poison that could paralyse completely!

CHAPTER EIGHT
The Great Mishasso

LIFTED ON THE backs of the strange, repellent spider-men, I was borne deep into the interior of the weird city.

Lighted by faintly luminous rocks, it was a labyrinth that seemed to have no plan or purpose to it.

We passed through corridors and chambers that sometimes seemed little more than conduits and on other occasions opened out into great, balconied halls.

I became convinced that this was not the work of the spider-men—not the work of men at all, but of some alien intelligence created, perhaps, by the effect of atomic radiation. That intelligence—half mad ever to have conceived this city—had probably perished long since, unless spider-men were their servants.

Somehow I thought not, because the corridors and halls were full of dirt, cobwebs and the decay of centuries. I paused to wonder just how these spider-men had come into being—whether they were cousins of the huge spiders I had seen outside. If they were related, what unholy union in the distant past had produced such fruit as these?

They scuttled along, bearing me in their strong arms. I did not dare speculate what fate had in store for me. I was convinced they intended to torture me, perhaps eat me in some ghastly rite—that I was, in fact, to be the fly in their parlour!

My guess was closer than I at first realized.

At length we entered an enormous hall, far bigger than anything else. It was dark and illuminated only by the dim radiance of the rock itself.

But now I could feel the drug beginning to wear off and I flexed my muscles experimentally—as much as was possible since the sticky web—drawn, I now guessed, from the actual bodies of the spider-men—still restricted my movement.

And then I saw it!

It was a vast web stretching across the hall. It shimmered in the faint light and I could just make out a figure spread-eagled in it. I was certain then that it was Hool Haji.

The spider-men themselves were evidently unaffected by their own sticky webs, for several of them began to haul me up strands of this web towards the other victim who was, I saw, indeed Hool Haji.

And there, hanging in space, they left us, scuttling away into the gloom on their furry legs. They had made not a sound since I had first encountered them.

My mouth was still stiff from the drug but I managed to say a few words. I had been placed below and to one side of Hool Haji and so could see little of him save his left foot and part of his calf.

"Hool Haji—can you speak?"

"Yes. Have you any indication what they intend to do with us, my friend?"

"No."

"I am sorry I led you into this, Michael Kane."

"It was not your fault."

"I should have been more cautious. If I had been we should all have been away by now. Is the aircraft safe?"

"As far as I know."

I began to test the web. The actual net in which I had been caught was becoming brittle and broken until I was at last able to fling out my hand. But my hand was immediately trapped immovably on the main web.

"I tried the same thing," Hool Haji said from above. "I can think of no possible means of escape."

I had to admit he was probably right, but I racked my brains nonetheless. I had begun to get a feeling that something horrible was in store for us unless I could devise a means of escape.

I began to try to work my other arm loose.

Then we heard the noise—a loud, scraping noise like the sound of the spider-men moving, but magnified greatly.

Looking down, we suddenly saw two huge eyes, at least four feet in diameter, looking unblinkingly up at us.

They were the eyes of a spider. My heard lurched.

Then a voice sounded—a soft, rustling, ironic voice which could only have issued from the owner of the eyes.

"Sso, an appetissing morssel for today'ss feasst…"

I was even more stunned to hear a voice coming from the creature.

"Who are you?" I demanded in a none too firm voice.

"I am Mishassa—the Great Mishassa, lasst of the folk of Shaas-sazheen."

"And those creatures—your minions?"

There came a sound that might have been an inhuman chuckle.

"My sspawn. Produced by experiments in the laboratories of Shaassazheen—the culmination of… But you would know your fate, would you not?"

I shuddered. I fancied that I guessed it already. I did not reply.

"Quake, little one, for you are to be my ssupper ssoon…"

Now I could see the creature more clearly. It was a giant spider—plainly one of many produced by the atomic radiation that had affected this part of the country all those thousands of years before.

Mishassa was slowly beginning to climb the web. I felt the thing sag as his weight went on to it.

I continued my effort to release my other arm and at last managed to free it of the net without trapping it on the web. I remembered the little skinning knife in my harness and decided I must try to reach that if I could.

Inch by inch I moved my hand towards the knife… Inch by inch…

At last my fingers gripped the haft and I eased the knife from its sheath.

The spider-beast was coming closer. I began to hack first at that part of the web holding my other arm.

I worked desperately but the web was tough. Then at last it parted and I was able, moving cautiously, to reach my sword.

I stretched my arm upwards and sliced away as much of the web around Hool Haji as I could reach, then turned again to face the giant spider.

Its voice whispered at me:

"You cannot esscape. Even if you were abssolutely free you would not esscape me—I am sstronger than you, sswifter than you..."

What he said was true—but it did not stop me trying!

Soon its horrible legs were only a few inches from me and I prepared to defend myself against it as best I could. Then I heard a yell from Hool Haji and saw his body fly past me and land squarely on the back of the spider-beast. He clung to its hair shouting for me to try to do the same.

I was only dimly aware of what he intended to do, but I leapt, too, breaking free of the last of the strands and dropping towards the spider-beast's back to land there and hang tightly with one hand to the weird fur. In my other hand I held my sword.

Hool Haji said, "Give me your sword—I am stronger than you."

I passed it to him and drew my knife.

The beast yelled in fury and shouted incomprehensible words at us as we began to hack at its back with our weapons.

It had probably been used to more passive offerings in the shape of its own minions—but we were two fighting men of Vashu and were prepared to sell our lives dearly before allowing ourselves to become a banquet for a big, talkative spider!

It hissed and cursed. It darted about in fury, dropping from web to ground. But still we clung on, still driving our weapons into it, seeking a vital spot.

It reared up and nearly toppled over so that we should have been crushed beneath its great bulk. But perhaps it had the instincts of the originals of the species—many of which, once on their backs, cannot get to their feet again. It recovered its balance just in time and began to scuttle backwards and forwards at random.

Sticky, black blood was spurting from a dozen wounds but none had, it appeared, been effective in slowing it down. Suddenly it began to run in a straight line, a thin, high wailing sound coming from it.

We lay flat as its speed increased, looking our puzzlement at one another.

It must have been moving at a good sixty miles an hour—probably more—as it darted along the tunnels, carrying us deeper and deeper into the city.

Now the wailing increased in volume. The spider-creature had gone berserk. Whether it was exhibiting a madness, a heritage of its mad ancestors that it had only now failed to control, or whether our wounds were driving it berserk with pain we were never to know.

Suddenly I saw movement ahead.

It was a pack of the spider-men—whether they were the same who had taken us to the hall of the web I could not guess—looking plainly panic-stricken as we rushed at them.

Then the huge, intelligent spider paused in its mad rush and began to fall on them, biting them to death, taking a head in its jaws and snapping it off at the neck, or biting a torso in two. It was a grisly sight.

We continued to cling as best we could to the furry back of the incensed beast. Occasionally it would shout a recognizable word or phrase but they made no sense to us.

Soon every single spider-man had been destroyed and nothing was left but a heap of dismembered corpses.

My arm was aching and I felt I could not hang on to the fur much longer. Any moment I was going to drop and become prey to the spider-beast. From Hool Haji's grim expression I could see that he, too, was feeling the strain and could not bear it much longer.

And then, quite suddenly, the spider-beast began to sag at the leg joints. The legs were slowly drawn up under its body and it sank down amongst the broken bodies of its servitors.

It had destroyed them, it seemed, in its death-throes, for it cried one word: "Gone!"—and died.

We made sure that the heart had ceased to beat and then virtually fell from the beast's back and stood looking up at it.

"I am glad it died and not us," I said, "but it must have realized it was the last survivor of its aberrant species. What actually went on in that crazed, alien brain, I wonder? I feel sorry for it in a way. Its death was somehow noble."

"You saw more than I did," Hool Haji broke in. "All I saw was an enemy that nearly destroyed us. But we have destroyed it—that is good."

This pragmatic statement from my friend shook me from my somewhat speculative frame of mind—possibly out of place in the circumstances—and made me begin to wonder how we were to find our way out of this maze of a city.

I wondered, also, if all the spider-men had been killed in the death-throes of the beast.

We picked our way through the ruin of corpses and followed the tunnel until it turned into a large hall.

We discovered a further tunnel leading off the hall and plodded on, simply hoping that we should eventually find a room with a window or exit—for there had been some visible from the outside.

The tunnels were difficult for Hool Haji to negotiate most of the time—only a few of them were large enough to take the spider-beast, for instance. This led me to conclude that the creature we had destroyed had been, even amongst his own kind, a 'sport.'

Once again something in me awakened sympathy for the misshapen creature that had been so ill-fitted for the world and yet plainly possessed an excellent intelligence. In spite of its having threatened my life, I could not hate it in any way.

It was while I was still in this philosophical mood that we stumbled upon the vats.

The first indication of their existence that we received was the smell. Breathing in the vapour, we felt a slight stiffness in our muscles. Then we entered a hall over which crude gangplanks had been placed, for the floor, which was sunken, was full of a noisome, bubbling fluid.

We paused beside the gangplank, looking down.

"I think I know what this is," I said to Hool Haji.

"The poison?"

"Exactly—the stuff which they coated on those needle-poles to paralyse us."

I frowned. "This could come in useful," I said.

"In what way?" my friend asked.

"I'm not sure—I have a feeling that it might. It will do no harm to take samples." I pointed to the far wall.

On the shelf stood several pottery flasks and a heap of poles with six-inch needles at their tips.

Carefully we crossed the vat by means of the gangplank, heading towards the shelf. We breathed in as little as possible for fear that our muscles would become paralysed altogether, causing us to plunge into the vat, and we should either drown or die from an overdose of the stuff.

At last we reached the shelf, feeling stiffer with every moment that passed. I took down two flasks of good, if weird, workmanship, and handed them to Hool Haji, who stooped and filled them. We rammed stoppers into the flasks and attached them to our belts, then we took a number of poles and left the hall of the vats by the nearest exit.

Now the floor of the tunnel rose and this gave us some hope.

I could see light glimmering from somewhere, though I could not see its direct source.

Just as we turned into a small passage and saw daylight coming through an irregular opening to one side of the passage, the light was momentarily blocked out by the sudden eruption into the place of a number of the large spiders I had seen earlier.

I drew my sword, which my blue friend had returned to me, and he used one of the poles to flail about him at the disgusting creatures. They paused only for a short time to attack us and then scuttled past, disappearing into the depths of the city.

What I had at first thought to be a direct attack was, in fact, nothing more than the nocturnal creatures returning to the darkness of the city.

We clambered out of the window and stood once again on what I can only call the "surface" or roof of the city—a place of unnatural cliffs and canyons all of the same darkly shining, obsidian stuff. It still looked as if it had been moulded whilst malleable rather than constructed in any fashion men would employ to build a city.

Our feet slipping on the smooth surfaces, we stumbled along, now realizing we had no real idea where our ship was in relation to us!

I imagine we would have wandered like this for many more hours—perhaps days—if we had not suddenly caught sight of Jil Deera's stocky figure framed against the jungle beyond. We yelled to him and waved.

He turned, his hand on his sword-hilt, his stance wary. Then he grinned as he recognized us.

"Where is Vas Oola?" I asked as we walked towards each other.

"He is still with the aircraft, guarding it," the warrior replied. "At least"—he looked distastefully around—"I hope he is."

"Why are you here?" asked Hool Haji.

"When you both did not return a nightfall I became worried. I thought you had been captured since I heard no sounds such as a wild beast might make, and as soon as it was dawn I set out on your trail—and found this place. Have you seen the creatures that inhabit it? Huge spiders!"

"You will find the remains of even stranger denizens below the surface somewhere," Hool Haji said laconically.

"I hope you left yourself markers for your way back," I said to Jil Deera, thinking myself a fool for not having done just that myself.

"I have." Jil Deera pointed into the jungle. "It is this way, come."

Since ill-luck had, for the most part, dogged us since we had left the haunt of the Yaksha, we were in some fear for the safety of our craft. We should have been in a far worse predicament, stranded on a land we had absolutely no knowledge of at all, if the balloon had been attacked and wrecked.

But it was quite safe and so was Vas Oola, who seemed very relieved to see us.

We had paused to cut small logs for use as ballast, and these were soon aboard.

Then, once aboard, we released the mooring lines and began to rise gently skywards.

As soon as we were high enough above the great jungle, which seemed to stretch away to every horizon, I started the engine, set our course and soon we were—or we hoped devoutly we were— on our way to Mendishar to see if something could be saved from the wreckage of the ill-fated revolution.

CHAPTER NINE
Sentenced to Die!

THANKFULLY WE CROSSED the ocean without mishap and arrived, at length, at the borders of Mendishar.

We landed in the hills and hid our craft.

Twice, as we scoured the hills in the hope of discovering some information, we came upon totally destroyed villages.

Once we were lucky. We met an old crone who had, by luck, escaped the destruction. She told us that whole families of hillpeople had been arrested; many, many villages razed and hundreds, possibly thousands, slain.

She told us that the leaders of the revolution who had been captured were due to die in a great ritual personally inaugurated by the upstart Bradhinak Jewar Baru. She did not know when, only that it had not yet taken place.

We decided we would have to visit the capital—Mendisharling—ourselves in order to see just what the true situation was, judge the mood of the populace and, if possible, rescue those under sentence of death.

With robes salvaged from one of the ruined villages, Hool Haji disguised himself as an itinerant trader and myself as—a bundle!

I, of course, would draw too much attention in whatever disguise I attempted, so I had to become the "trader's" goods!

It was in this manner, slung over Hool Haji's shoulder, that I entered, for the first time, the capital city of Mendishar. It was a place of little spirit. Peeping through a small rent in the cloth in which I was swathed I could see that, apart from the swaggering, boorish Priosa, there was not a back that was not bent, not a face that was not lined with misery, not a child that was not emaciated.

We passed through the market and there was little of anything nourishing on sale.

The whole city had an air of desolation about it which contrasted sharply with the bright uniforms of the "chosen" Priosa.

It was a scene familiar to me from my reading, but I had never seen anything like it in real life. It was a place ruled by a tyrant who so feared for his own security that he did not dare relax his iron rule for a single moment.

Whatever happened now, I reflected as I was humped along by my friend—who was not, I felt, going out of his way to make my ride comfortable—the tyrant must fall eventually, for people can be ground down only for so long. At some time the tyrant—or his descendant—relaxes, and it is at that moment his subjects choose to act!

Hool Haji took a room at a tavern near the square and went to it at once. Then he placed me on the hard bed and sat down mopping his brow as I disentangled myself from the cloth.

I grimaced as I sat up.

"I feel as if every bone in my body is dislocated," I said.

"I apologize." Hool Haji smiled. "But it would look suspicious if an impoverished trader like myself should treat his goods as if they were precious things instead of the few skins and rolls of fabric he told the gate guards he had."

"I suppose you're right," I agreed, trying to wriggle the circulation back into my legs and arms. "What now?"

"You wait here while I go about the city and see what information I can glean—and test the temper of the people. If they are ready to rise up against Jewar Baru—as I suspect they might be, given the right push—then perhaps we can decide a means of destroying Jewar Baru's rule."

He set off almost at once, leaving me to do little more than fiddle with my fingers. The reason I had come with him—apart from the obvious one of being his friend and ally—was that if he was captured I might have a chance of taking the news back to our friends and because, if we needed the airship, I would be able to operate it in the event of this happening.

I waited and waited until, in the late afternoon, I heard a disturbance in the street below.

Cautiously I went to the window and peeped out.

Hool Haji was down there talking heatedly to a couple of insolent-looking Priosa guards.

"I am simply a poor trader," he was saying. "Nothing more or less, gentlemen."

"You answer closely the description we have of the Pretender Hool Haji. He fled, coward that he was, from a village we investigated some weeks ago, leaving his followers to fight for him. We are seeking this weakling since he has managed to convince a few misguided people that his rule will be better for Mendishar than that of the noble Bradhi Jewar Baru."

"He sounds a wretch," Hool Haji said dutifully. "A positive scoundrel. I hope you catch him, noble sirs. Now I must return..."

"We believe that you are this *hwok'kak* Hool Haji," one guard said, blocking Hool Haji's path and using one of the most insulting terms in the Martian vocabulary. Literally, a hwok'kak is a reptile of particularly filthy habits, but the implications of this are far wider and impossible to describe here.

Hool Haji controlled himself visibly on hearing this, but probably gave himself away—not that there seemed any chance of the guards letting him come back to the tavern.

"You will come with us for questioning," said the second guard. "And if you are not Hool Haji you will probably be released— though the Bradhi has no love for rabble such as wandering traders."

There was nothing for it, I decided, but to act. There was a spare sword in the roll of cloth—it had been trying to stab me all the way through the city. I went to the bed and tugged the sword free, then returned to my position at the window.

Now was the time to try to help my friend, for once the whole city was alerted to stop Hool Haji escaping there would be little chance of us leaving Mendisharling alive.

I balanced myself momentarily on the window sill and then launched myself with a yell at the nearest guard.

The great warrior was astonished to see what was, to him, a tiny man leaping at him with a naked sword.

I landed only a short distance from him and immediately engaged him.

Realizing that my decision had been the only sensible one and that secrecy was no longer possible, Hool Haji attacked the second guard.

Soon the street had cleared as if by magic and only the two Priosa and ourselves were left, battling to the death.

I hoped that the downtrodden populace did not have spies among them who would go and bring other Priosa. If we could finish these, we might just make it from the city.

My opponent was still baffled. He never really recovered his wits. Within a few minutes I had stabbed him through the side of his armour and he lay dead on the cobbles of the street.

Hool Haji also finished his opponent quickly. We turned at the sound of running feet and saw a whole detachment of Priosa coming towards us. Mounted on a great grey dahara was a tall, heavily built Mendishar in golden armour.

"*Jewar Baru!*" The name was an oath on Hool Haji's lips.

Plainly these warriors had not been summoned but had heard the sound of our fight from close by.

Hool Haji prepared to stand his ground, but I tugged at his arm.

"Don't be a fool, friend. You will be overwhelmed in an instant! Leave now and we will return soon to deal out justice to the tyrant."

Reluctantly, Hool Haji followed me as I ducked back into the tavern and barred the door.

Almost at once the guards were battering at the door and we ran upstairs to the third and top storey of the building, and from there through a hatchway on to the roof.

The houses in this quarter of the city were huddled close together and there was no difficulty in leaping from one flat roof to another.

Behind us the guards—but not Jewar Baru, who had doubtless remained in the safety of the street—had reached the roof and were following us, shouting at us to stop.

I do not think they recognized Hool Haji at that stage—although it was well-known by then that he had a man like myself as a constant fighting companion—and would probably have exerted themselves even more if they had realized just who my friend was.

The roofs became lower now and at last we were running across the tops of single-storey buildings.

Near the city wall we dropped back into the street. People were startled at our appearance and we were in time to see a couple of half-drunk Priosa come out of a wine shop and stagger towards their daharas.

We were there first, mounting the beasts, as it were under their noses, wheeled them about and were off, heading for the gate, leaving the shouting guards still confused.

Near the gates we met four Priosa who possessed faster reactions than their friends. Seeing us on what were evidently stolen mounts they tried to block our path.

Our swords swung swiftly and we left two dead behind us and the two others wounded as we rode hell for leather through the gates and down the long road that led away from Mendisharling.

Already riders were pursuing us as we galloped along the trail and then turned sharply towards the hills on our left.

Into the hills we rode, our enemies close behind us, our beasts beginning to flag.

If night had not fallen soon I think we should have had to turn and fight a force that was far too large to give us any hope. But night did fall and we were able to elude our pursuers before the rising of the moons.

In the comparative safety of a cave we had discovered, Hool Haji told me all he had learned in the city.

The people were beginning to murmur almost openly against the tyrant, but were too frightened to do anything about it—and too disorganized for it to be effective if they did.

He thought that the news of the wanton razing of villages and killing of the innocent had filtered through to the city, though the Priosa were making every attempt to discount the rumours.

Nearly two hundred prisoners of all ages and sexes were even now languishing in Jewar Baru's jails—ready for the great "sacrifice" to be held in the city square.

All of these had received the death sentence for their supposed aiding of Hool Haji and his supporters. Some of them had known nothing of it—and the children, of course, had no part at all. This was Jewar Baru's example. It would be a bloody example. It might enable him to continue to hold the people down for another two or three years at most—but surely no longer.

"But that is not the point," I said to Hool Haji. "These people must somehow be saved—*now*."

"Of course," he agreed. "And do you know the name of one of those in Jewar Baru's jail—the man of whom they intend to make a particular example?"

"Who?"

"Morahi Vaja. He was captured in the fighting. There were special orders to take him alive!"

"When is this "sacrifice" to take place?" I asked.

Hool Haji put his head in his hands.

"Tomorrow at midday," he groaned. "Oh, Michael Kane, what can we do? How can we stop this happening?"

"There is only one thing we can do," I said grimly. "We must make use of the resources we have. The four of us—you, myself, Jil Deera and Vas Oola—must attack Mendisharling!"

"How can four men attack a great city?" he asked incredulously.

"I will tell you how the attack can be made," I told him, "but there is only a small chance of it succeeding."

"Tell me your plan," he said.

CHAPTER TEN
A Desperate Scheme

I STOOD AT the controls of the airship and stared through a porthole at the countryside ahead.

The three blue giants behind me said nothing. There was nothing to say. Our plan, a simple one, had already been fully discussed.

It was close on midday and we were making rapidly for Mendisharling. The plan depended primarily on the timing. If we failed, then at least our failure would be spectacular and might at least point the way for future revolutionaries.

The towers of the capital were now in sight. The city was decorated as if for a festival. Banners flew from every tower and mast—a gay occasion, a stranger would have thought. We knew better...

In the city square stood two hundred stakes. Tied to the stakes were two hundred prisoners—men, women and children. Standing by them, with sacrificial knives ready in their hands, were two hundred splendidly dressed Priosa.

In the centre of these circles of stakes, on a platform, stood Jewar Baru himself, clad in his golden armour and carrying a golden knife in his hand. Also on the dais was a stake. Tied to it was Morahi Vaja, his face set, his eyes staring out at nothing but his own terrible fate.

Surrounding the square, ordered there by decree of the upstart Bradhi, was the entire populace of Mendisharling, many rows deep.

Jewar Baru stood with arms raised sunwards, a cruel, nervous smile twitching his thin lips. He was waiting in ghoulish anticipation for the sun to reach its zenith.

There was silence in the square save for the puzzled murmurings of the young children, both in the crowd and at the stake, who did not know what was about to happen. Their parents hushed them but did not explain. How could they explain?

Jewar Baru's eyes were still fixed on the sun as he began to speak.

"Oh, Mendishar, there are those among you who followed the Great Dark One and chose to go against the decrees of the Great Light One whose material manifestation is the Life Giver, the sun. Moved by wretched motives of self-importance and evil, they sent for the murderer and coward Hool Haji to lead them in revolution against your chosen Bradhi. Out of the depths of the dark wastelands came the interloper, out of the night, to fight against the Priosa, the Children of the Sky, the Sons of the Great Light One. But the Great Light One sent a sign to Jewar Baru and told him what was intended, and Jewar Baru went to fight against Hool Haji, who fled and will never be seen again in the daytime, for he is a skulker in the night. Thus the coward fled and the Great Light triumphed. His followers are here today. They will be sacrificed to the Great Light not in a spirit of vengeance, but as a gift to He Who Watches—the Great Light—so that Mendishar may be purified and the death of these will wash away *our* guilt."

The response to this superstitious hypocrisy was not enthusiastic.

Jewar Baru turned towards Morahi Vaja, his golden knife raised over the warrior's heart, ready to cut it from him in the blood ritual.

The atmosphere was tense. Jewar Baru's sacrifice of Morahi Vaja would be the signal for two hundred knives to rip out two hundred innocent hearts!

The sun was only a few moments from its zenith as Jewar Baru began his incantation.

He was halfway through it and in a state of near-trance when the airship arrived, unnoticed until now, over the city. All eyes were on Jewar Baru, or else were covered—though he had decreed that all must see.

This is what we had counted on—why we had timed the arrival so carefully even though it would give us only a few seconds in which to try and save the victims in the square.

We had cut the engines and were drifting over the square, falling lower and lower.

Then our shadow crossed Jewar Baru's dais just as he was about to plunge the knife into Morahi Vaja's body.

He wheeled and looked up. All other eyes followed his gaze.

Jewar Baru's eyes widened in astonishment.

It was then, from within the cabin, that I raised my arm and flung what I was holding at the upstart Bradhi.

As I had planned, the point of the javelin grazed his throat—but it was sufficient.

Jewar Baru, as if struck rigid by the power of some godlike being, became paralysed in the position he had been when looking up at us.

For the moment we were fighting superstition with superstition so that the appearance of our ship over the square would look like the visitation of some angry god.

Early that morning I had manufactured a crude megaphone and I now bellowed through this, my voice distorted and magnified more by the echoes from the surrounding buildings.

"People of Mendishar, your tyrant is struck down—strike down his minions!"

The populace began to murmur and their mood was plainly angry as well as puzzled—though the anger was not directed at us. It had been a move depending on psychology. We guessed that the paralysis of Jewar Baru would make his followers lose heart and give heart to the ordinary people.

Slowly the crowd began to move inward towards the centre of the square while the Priosa, who began to look round in a panicky way, were drawing their swords.

I brought the airship closer to the dais, giving Hool Haji a chance to leap from ship to platform and stand beside his frozen enemy.

"Hool Haji!" gasped Morahi Vaja from where he was tied to the stake.

"Hool Haji!" This came from several Priosa who had recognized the exiled prince.

"Hool Haji!" This from those folk of Mendisharling who had heard the name spoken by the Priosa.

"Yes—Hool Haji!" cried my friend, raising his sword high. "Jewar Baru would have it that I am a coward who deserts his people. But see—I enter his city all but single-handed to save my friends and tell you to depose him now! Strike down the Priosa who have persecuted you for so long. Now is your chance to avenge yourselves!"

For a moment there was virtual silence. Then began a murmur which grew gradually louder and louder until it became a roar.

Then the entire populace of Mendisharling was moving in on the terrified Priosa.

Many folk died beneath the swinging swords of the soldiers before the Priosa finally went down beneath the sheer weight of numbers. But fewer—far fewer—died than would have died in the sacrifice, or later in Jewar Baru's jails.

We watched as the tide of humanity engulfed the Priosa in what appeared to be a single fluid action. When it was over—in the short space of a few minutes—not one Priosa who had been prepared to sacrifice a victim that day was left alive. Indeed, few of the corpses were whole. They had literally been torn to pieces. A fitting, if bloody, end.

I had missed joining in the action, but our plan had been based entirely on judging the mood of the people, the psychological effect our appearance would have, and the result of my poison-tipped spear—smeared with the paralysing stuff we had found in the vats of the City of the Spider—on Jewar Baru. If our plan had failed we should have been destroyed in as short a time as were our enemies.

I was trembling both with reaction and relief as I swung down a rope-ladder to stand beside my friends on the dais. We cut

Morahi Vaja free. Down in the square, all around us, the other reprieved victims were being released.

A great cheer now rose up for Hool Haji.

It lasted for many, many minutes. Meanwhile Jill Deera and Vas Oola swung from the ship and moored her to the stake.

I stepped forward and cried to the people of Mendishar: "Salute your Bradhi—Hool Haji! Do you accept him?"

"*We do!*" came back the voice of the crowd.

Hool Haji raised his hand, moved by this response.

"Thank you. I have saved you from the rule of the tyrant and helped you overcome him and his followers—though the true saviour is Michael Kane. But now you must seek out the rest of the Priosa and capture them, for they must all pay the penalty for their deeds over the past years. Go now—arm yourselves with the weapons of your persecutors and scour the streets for those who still live!"

The men began to stoop and pick up the swords of the fallen Priosa. Then they were rushing through the streets and soon the sounds of conflict echoed again in Mendisharling.

As the effect of the poison was beginning to wear off, we bound Jewar Baru securely.

He was mumbling now and foam flicked his lips. He was plainly quite mad—had been mad for some time, but this sudden defeat had tipped the balance completely.

"What do you intend to do with him?" I asked Hool Haji.

"Try and kill him," said my friend simply.

Now I had a feeling of anticlimax. It was over—our object had been achieved rapidly. Again a sense of aimlessness overcame me.

We established ourselves in Jewar Baru's palace—the building which had housed generations of Hool Haji's ancestors before the populace had misguidedly followed the upstart to their own downfall.

Morahi Vaja took charge of the parties seeking out the Priosa who had escaped the initial coup. He left, but returned shortly to tell us that a great many of the Priosa were still out on patrol or else had fled the city. It would take time to locate them all—and many might well escape.

This gave me an idea. Although doubtless the Priosa who remained uncaught offered no real threat to Hool Haji, they should not be allowed to go unpunished. Their crimes were manifold—the sadistic killing of the innocent looming large among them.

This would be something in which I could help, I decided.

"I will be your scout," I said. "If I take the airship I will be able to travel much faster than the Priosa and work out their exact positions, and so on. Then I can return and tell you roughly where to find those who have escaped."

"A good plan," Hool Haji nodded. "I would come with you, but there are too many things still to be done here. Start in the morning—you need a little rest."

I saw the sense of this. A bedroom was placed at my disposal and I was soon asleep.

Next morning I climbed into my ship, waved to Hool Haji and told him that I would probably be away a few days. The great body of the Priosa, I was told, had fled south, so that would be the best direction in which to go.

The near-silent engine began to pulse, the propellers began to turn, and soon I had left Mendisharling and Hool Haji behind.

I did not realize then what fate—which has, I feel, taken an inordinate interest in my affairs—had in store for me.

CHAPTER ELEVEN
The Flying Monster

TWO DAYS LATER I was very far south indeed. I had seen several small bands of Priosa and noted their positions and the general direction which they were heading.

I had gone past the borders of Mendishar and saw in the distance a range of tall, black mountain peaks that seemed familiar.

Having, I felt, located all the Priosa I was likely to find, I decided to investigate the mountains and see if these were indeed what I suspected.

The mountains were what I had thought. The Mountains of Argzoon where earlier—or was it yet to happen?—I had fought against the minions of that wicked renegade Horguhl, and the beast which she had somehow hypnotically controlled.

I felt emotion stir in me—a sense almost of nostalgia—as I flew over those bleak mountains. I felt no love for the mountains themselves, of course, but they reminded me of my earlier adventures on Vashu and, more particularly, of the short period of happiness I had enjoyed with that beautiful girl Shizala. It was difficult to convince myself that she was as yet unborn.

I wondered if it would be worth flying down, but reasoned that the Argzoon had not yet been defeated and were likely to make short work of me. Then I would die for nothing.

I was just turning the ship when I saw the thing suddenly appear from a dark gorge and come flapping up towards me.

It was a monster of such astounding proportions that at first I believed it must be some weird kind of flying machine. Nothing could lift that bulk off the ground, let alone fly so swiftly, but a man-made device, I thought.

But it was not man-made.

It had the appearance of a two-headed heela—the small, savage beast that inhabited the forest further south—with great fangs and blazing eyes. From its shoulders sprouted vast, leathery wings. It was evidently a cousin of the heela in appearance and temperament. The heela was dangerous enough, but this creature was many times its size.

It was flying towards me, great taloned paws outstretched as if to seize me, both mouths of both heads gaping wide.

I rammed over the speed lever to 'full' and pulled another lever to let the ballast out of its cradles slung beneath the main cabin.

Climbing rapidly, I managed to put some extra distance between the beast and myself. But now the creature was gaining height and speed also.

I had not had time to turn the ship and was still heading almost due south. I wished for some weapon other than the poison-tipped lances still in the cabin and my sword. A machine-gun loaded with dumdum bullets might have had some slight effect on the beast. Better still, a large, rapid-fire artillery piece or a bazooka, or a flame-thrower, or one of those laser-projectors…

I had nothing of the sort. I was beginning to feel that I did not even have speed on my side as the monster clung to its trail and began slowly to shorten the distance between us.

The airship was not the most manœuvrable of craft, but the aerobatics I managed to perform would have astounded anyone who knew anything about the possibilities of manipulating a balloon-type vessel!

Below me—far, far below—I saw the heela forest that I had ventured through once with Darnad, Shizala's brother.

Then I was past that and still travelling due south.

I strained every ounce of energy from the motor so that I feared the propellers must shake themselves loose sooner or later.

Nearer and nearer flapped the monster. It was larger—including its vast wings—than my ship and I knew that a couple of rips from its claws alone could destroy the gas-bag and send me dropping like a stone to the ground far below.

It refused to give up. Surely, I thought, any ordinary animal would have tired by now. But no. Doggedly it pursued me, sensing perhaps that victory and a meal were in sight—though I could only feel he would be disappointed in the meal.

I circled higher. Soon, unless I was careful, I would be in an atmosphere too thin in breathe. Then I would no longer need to worry about the flying heela—or indeed about anything. I would be dead.

I wondered if, for all its ferocity, this creature were as cowardly as its smaller, land-bound cousins of the forests. If it were, there might be a way to scare it.

I racked my brains but could think of nothing. What *did* scare a two-headed flying mammal of several tons in sheer weight? The humorous answer presented itself—*another*, larger, two headed flying mammal! I had no such ally, however.

Now the heela—or whatever it was called—was much closer so that I could make out its features clearly.

By reflex more than by anything else, I reached for one of the poison-tipped lances and flung it through the port-hole at the thing.

I think it must have entered one of its throats, for the mouth closed, chewed—and there was no longer a spear. Now it was almost upon me and I decided that I might as well die fighting, however futilely.

I flung another spear, this time missing altogether. What happened next was astonishing. The beast reached out and snapped the falling spear in its mouth. Again it chewed, again it swallowed.

I felt chagrin then. It was not only unaffected by my puny weapons—it was enjoying them as a meal!

The spears served to slow it a little, at any rate, as it paused to snap them up! I flung the rest, trying for one of its eyes, but failed miserably.

The last thing I remembered was the beast finally catching up with the ship! A huge black shadow seemed to engulf me. I remember a ripping noise and realizing that I was doomed along with my ship—either to being eaten, gas-bag, cabin and all, in mid-air by a predator that seemed literally omnivorous, or to fall thousands of feet and be smashed to small fragments on the ground.

The cabin swung crazily and I fell back, hit my head on the side of the control panel and, as dizziness overcame me, I remember thinking that at least I would not be aware of my own dying.

CHAPTER TWELVE
New Friends

I FELT THAT every bone in my body was broken. As it happened—though every bone should have been—not one was! I was badly bruised and cut—that was all.

But where was I?

Alive? Just about. How? I could not guess.

I began to disentangle myself from the contents of the cabin. As far as I could tell it was not badly damaged—that building material of the Yaksha must be incredible stuff.

I got the hatch—which was above me now—open and crawled out into the comparative darkness of the Martian night, lit as it was by the twin moons.

The gas-bag bobbed on the ground, half empty. Had I dropped so rapidly that, once having released much of the contents of the gas-bag, the heela had been unable to follow me?

I did not know, but my tentative answer as to how I was saved was not very convincing.

I went back into the cabin, repressing a groan of pain from my bruising, and got a patch and a tin of the sticky substance we had found in the Yaksha city. Helium was still escaping from the bag but only slowly, since it had folded in on itself, forming a kind of pocket from which the gas was seeping less quickly than it would normally have done.

Hastily I patched the balloon and reflected thankfully that there were still enough spare tanks of helium to fill it.

Just as I was finishing my work I saw something to my right. It was a large object.

I approached it cautiously—and discovered the monster! How had it died? I stepped forward to see if I could tell—and then realized that it was still breathing!

Breathing with difficulty, to be sure, but breathing nonetheless!

I guessed that it had swallowed too much of the paralysing poison even for its incredible digestive system to absorb. In the act of attacking me it had been seized by paralysis and had veered away, flopping earthwards to land here. My damaged balloon must have followed it down and landed near it shortly afterwards.

I thanked providence for giving the heela its weird appetite. Then I ran back to the ship for my sword, which must have fallen from my belt as I hurtled downwards.

While the beast slept—and feeling something of a coward, though the creature needed to be slain lest it attack any other traveller—I pierced its faceted eyes, hoping that I had reached the brain. It threshed about, flinging me off twice, but I persevered until finally it was dead.

Then I returned to the airship and attached containers of helium to the valve of the bag.

I soon felt little worse, except for my bruises.

I decided to sleep in the cabin, having moored the ship to the ground, and try to get my bearings in the morning.

Still rather dazed and wearied from the previous day's experience, I took the air next morning without quite knowing what I planned.

Below me now I saw a broad river winding. I did not recognize the countryside at all, but decided to follow the river in the hope that I would spy some settlement on it where I could ask just where I was.

I followed this river, as it happened, for four days without sighting a single settlement.

When I eventually did see something it was not a settlement— but a fleet!

There were some dozen or so finely made sailing galleys of graceful beauty beating up the river. Flying lower, I saw that the ships were crewed by men like myself, only darker skinned.

I began to drop down towards the leading galley which, judging by the size and decoration of its single, lateen-rigged sail, was the flagship.

I caused some consternation before I found my megaphone and shouted down:

"I mean you no harm. Who are you?"

In the common language of Mars, though in an accent that was only barely familiar, one of the men shouted up:

"We are men of Mishim Tep bound for the Jewelled City! Who are you?"

Mishim Tep! That was Karnala's oldest ally—and Karnala was the land from where my Shizala came. I felt I was among friends!

I replied that I was a traveller from the North—a tribeless man who would welcome company if I were allowed to board the ship.

Their curiosity now seemed to be aroused and they also believed me when I said I offered no danger. So they allowed me to tether the balloon to their mast and descend my rope ladder to the deck—a difficult operation which, I pride myself, I accomplished with some dexterity.

The young captain, a pleasant warrior called Vorum Saz Hazhi, told me that he had been away for many months on an expedition to the coast, where a small ally of Mishim Tep's had been plagued by raiders. They had destroyed the raiders and were now on their way home to Mih-Sa-Voh, the Jewelled City, capital of Mishim Tep.

Rather than complicate matters, there and then I told him that I was a scientist, inventor of the airship we now had in tow, looking for commissions in the south. I said that I had journeyed from the Western continent—which was, strictly speaking, true.

"If you could invent *that*," Vorum Saz Hazhi said enthusiastically, "then you will be more than welcome at the court of our Bradhi and you need not fear going hungry. He will give you all the commissions you need."

I was pleased to hear that and made up my mind on the spot to set myself up as what I had said I was—a free-lance scientist!

I was not too worried about the Priosa I had failed to report. The mission had only been to occupy my time really, and the Priosa would probably be tracked down soon enough. I would, of course, return to Mendishar soon to ensure Hool Haji that I was safe. But, in the meanwhile, I could not resist the prospect of dwelling for a short while with people of my own size and general appearance—people, moreover, who had strong affinities of custom and tradition with my adopted nation, the Karnala.

Some days later the towers of the Jewelled city came in sight.

It was the most magnificent place I have seen in my life. Every tower and roof was decorated with precious or semi-precious gems so that from a distance the city looked like one vast blaze of scintillating colour.

Its harbour was made of white marble in which crystals sparkled, reflected in the dancing water of the river. A bright sun shone from a clear blue sky, the scents of shrubs and herbs were sweet, the sight and sound of happy, intelligent and well-cared-for people was a joy to my senses.

Many folk had come to welcome the arrival of the ships after their long expedition. They were dressed in bright cloaks which matched the brave display of banners from our masts. Many gasped to see the airship in tow.

The delicate music of the Southern Martians began to sound in the air, welcoming the return of the fleet. The sun was warm, the scene peaceful. It was the first time since I had arrived on Mars again that I had felt close to happiness.

Although Hool Haji and the Mendishar had been cultured and noble people, their civilization had had a touch of savagery about it, a faint echo of their links with their cousins the Argzoon, which the societies of the South did not possess. More than this, the Mendishar, like the Argzoon, were physically so strange to me that the feeling of being among men of my own breed again was good.

We set foot on the quay and Vorum Saz Hazhi's relatives came forward to greet him. He introduced me and they said I was welcome to be their guest until I could find a place of my own.

Vorum Saz Hazhi said that on the morrow he would seek an audience with the Bradhi.

Looking around the dock I saw that there were many warriors— more than I had noticed at first. Also there seemed to be hasty preparations in progress. Vorum Saz Hazhi noticed this too and was as puzzled as I was. He asked his parents about it.

They frowned and said first we must return home, then they would tell him the bad news.

It was not until evening, when we sat at table, that Vorum Saz Hazhi's parents began to tell him that Mishim Tep was preparing for war.

"It is a black day and I cannot understand how it should have happened," my new friend's father said. "But..."

Just then a man and a woman entered. They were about the same age as Vorum Saz Hazhi's parents. They wanted to learn all about the balloon, hear about my adventures and so on.

Thus the talk went away from politics as I politely told of my experiences in the North and on the Western continent. By the time the guests had left I was very much ready for bed and wasted no time using the room which the young warrior's parents had prepared for me.

In the morning Vorum Saz Hazhi went to the palace, where he was to be congratulated by the Bradhi for his victories, and I went to the harbour. We had arranged that he should speak to the Bradhi on my behalf while I was getting the balloon. Already the news would have reached the Bradhi, of course, but he would plainly want to see my ship for himself. I was to steer it to the palace and moor it there.

While making my way slowly to the harbour, dawdling a little— for I had plenty of time to spare—to look in shops and chat with those citizens of Mih-Sa-Voh who recognized me as the pilot of what was, to them, a marvelous flying machine, I saw a small procession pass me.

It consisted of tired-looking warriors mounted on dahara. They had evidently just come back, also, from an expedition, for they were dusty and bore minor wounds.

They had a prisoner—a wild looking man with a long, thick beard and very blond, long matted hair. He, too, bore many recent scars and had his hands tied behind him as he sat his dahara.

In spite of his savage appearance, he bore himself well. Although I dismissed the idea as a trick of the mind, I was sure there was something about him very familiar to me. Since that seemed impossible, I refused to waste my energy trying to puzzle out why I should feel this, but I asked a passer-by if he knew who the prisoner was.

The man shook his head. "Doubtless one of our enemies—though that is not their normal appearance."

I continued on to the harbour and found my balloon still waiting for me, now moored to one of several iron rings in quayside.

I climbed into the cabin and started the engine—that marvellous little unit which seemed to require no fuel.

Then I steered just above the roof-tops of the sparkling City of Jewels towards the palace, a large building that was more magnificent than any of the rest. It seemed literally built of precious gems!

I had learned that many kinds of jewels were mined in Mishim Tep and, though they were useful trading commodities, no special value was placed on them by the populace.

I reached the palace steps and dropped down a little to where guards ran forward at my shouted instructions to take my mooring lines and make them fast.

Vorum Saz Hazhi now appeared at the top of the steps and greeted me as I mounted the steps.

"I have told the Bradhi of your offer," he said, "and he would interview you now. He thinks that you have come at an opportune moment—ships like this could be useful in fighting our enemies."

As I joined him I noticed that he looked worried.

"What troubles you?" I asked.

He took my arm as he led me into the palace. "I do not know," he said. "Perhaps it is the cares of this terrible war we are about to mount, but the Bradhi does not seem himself. There is something strange going on and I cannot think what it can be."

That was all he had a chance to say for then the huge jewelled doors of the throne room were opened and I saw a vast hall, lined with great, colourful banners and with tiers of galleries stretching up to the roof, high above, and the walls flanked with nobles, men and women, all looking towards me in polite curiosity.

On the throne dais at the far end were three figures. The Bradhi was in the middle, a care-worn man with grey-streaked hair and a massive, impressive head that seemed carved from rock.

On his left, his hands still bound, stood the wild man I had seen earlier.

But it was the person who sat on a stool beside the Bradhi whom I recognized—and recognized with loathing. Yet, at the same time, that person's presence aroused in me a feeling of jubilation.

It was Horguhl, that evil woman who had, both directly and indirectly, been the cause of most of my troubles on my first trip to Mars.

Horguhl!

This could only mean that my calculations about time had been right, even if I had slipped up slightly on those about space.

If Horguhl was here then, somewhere, so was Shizala!

Both Horguhl and the wild man turned to look at me. And they both spoke at once, saying the same two words:

"Michael Kane!"

Why had they both recognized me?

CHAPTER THIRTEEN
Horguhl's Treachery

I ADVANCED NO further, aware that I was in danger.

And then, suddenly, I recognized the wild man's voice and knew why he had seemed so familiar to me. It was Darnad—Shizala's brother with whom I had parted what seemed years before in the Caverns of Argzoon.

If he was a prisoner then it was my duty to free him, for he was a close friend.

I drew my sword and instead of turning and running for the hall ran towards Darnad before the astonished courtiers could act.

Horguhl was screaming and pointing to me. "That is the one—that is he! He is the sole cause of this war!"

How I, in my absence in another time and space, could have caused a war, I did not pause to work out. I cut Darnad's bonds and then wheeled as a courtier came at me with his sword.

Using a trick taught me as a boy by my old fencing master, M. Clarchet, I hooked the tip of my sword in the basket-hilt of his, flipped the weapon out of his hand and sent it spinning towards me. Then I flung it to Darnad—and we were both armed. The trick would not have worked on anyone but a man taken off his guard—but it had worked and that was the important thing.

The whole throne room was in confusion. I was sure that there was some awful mistake and that Horguhl was responsible for it, and I did not want to kill any of the folk who had treated me so hospitably.

Darnad and I fought a defensive action from our corner of the throne dais and the courtiers were cautious about attacking us too hard in case their Bradhi should be wounded.

This gave me an idea for a bluff which would prevent any blood being spilt—including ours.

I leapt behind the Bradhi and seized the man by his harness. Then I raised my sword above his head.

"Harm us—and you slay your Bradhi," I said in a loud, clear voice.

They paused and lowered their weapons.

"Do not listen to him," Horguhl screamed at them. "He lies, he will not kill your Bradhi!"

I spoke as sternly as I could—though Horguhl, knowing me better than they did, was perfectly right in what she had said—and addressed the courtiers.

"I am a desperate man," I said. "I do not know why you should hold the son of the ruler of your oldest ally a prisoner or why you should allow this evil woman to occupy the throne-dais of your Bradhi. But, since you do, I must protect myself and my friend. Do you not recognize him as Darnad of the Karnala, Bradhinak and Pukan-Nara?"

"We do!" one courtier shouted. "And that is why we hold him! We are at war with the Karnala!"

"At war?" I could hardly believe my ears. "At war with your friends since the ancient days? Why?"

"I will tell you why," screamed Horguhl. "And you should know, since you were partly the cause of all this. Your wanton Bradhinaka Shizala had the Bradhi's son, Telem Fas Ogdai, damned and murdered so that she might marry—*you!*"

I was astounded at the enormity of the lie. It was Horguhl who had been responsible for Telem Fas Ogdai turning traitor and eventually being killed in fair fight.

"Surely it is common knowledge that Telem Fas Ogdai betrayed Karnala?" I said, turning to the courtiers. But they groaned and muttered, unconvinced by what I had said.

Their spokesman said: "She has told us the whole despicable plot that you and Shizala of the Karnala devised between you. The honour of Mishim Tep has been affronted, her favourite son destroyed, the Bradhi attacked and humiliated—these are things only blood can wipe out!"

"You speak nonsense!" I said. "I know the truth—Horguhl has hypnotized you as she has hypnotized so many before. You believe a story that would not stand up to analysis for a moment if your minds had not been dulled by her power."

The Bradhi struggled in my grasp. "If it had not been for her we should never have known the truth," he said. He spoke mechanically and I was sure that he was totally in Horguhl's power.

"Your Bradhi has been mesmerized by her!" I said desperately.

"You lie!" Horguhl screamed. "I am only a simple woman who was deceived by Michael Kane just as he tries to deceive you. Kill him! Kill him!"

"How can one woman have convinced a whole nation of an enormous lie?" I shouted, turning to her. "What have you done, you evil creature? You have set two great nations at each other's throats. Have you no sense of shame for what you do?"

Although she continued to act her part, I saw a glimmer of irony in her eyes as she replied. "Have *you* no sense of shame? You interloper who trampled on all the great customs and traditions of the Southern nations in order to have the woman you loved."

I could see that convincing them was impossible.

"Very well," I said. "If I am the villain you say I am, then you know that I will carry out my threat and slay the Bradhi if you try to attack me." I began to move forward and she stepped reluctantly backward to let me pass.

Darnad covered my back as we went through the hall towards the doors and thence through the entrance chamber to the palace steps and my airships.

I forced the Bradhi to climb the ladder and Darnad followed me. Once inside the cabin I turned to the old man.

"You must believe us when we deny what Horguhl has said," I told him urgently.

"Horguhl always speaks the truth," he said in a flat voice, his eyes glassy.

"Do you not realize that she has hypnotized you?" I asked him. "The Karnala and the men of Mishim Tep have been friends for so long that a war between them could destroy everything that Southern culture stands for!"

"She would not lie."

"But she *does* lie!" Darnad spoke now for the first time. "I do not understand everything of which you speak, but I do understand that neither my sister nor Michael Kane would ever do the things of which you accuse them."

"Horguhl is good. She tells the truth."

I shook my head sadly. Then I led him towards the hatch and showed him the ladder.

"You may go, you poor deluded thing," I said. "Is this that I see—the shadow of a once-great Bradhi?"

Something seemed to spark in his eyes for a moment and I could see the kind of man he really was when not in Horguhl's hypnotic power. Grief for his son's treachery and death must have sapped his powers for a time—and in that time Horguhl had managed to reach him and work on his mind until his will was submerged.

I had underestimated her. I had thought her defeated in the Caverns of Argzoon but instead she had immediately hit upon a scheme to gain her ends and revenge herself on all her enemies—and one of those enemies, though they did not realize it, was Mishim Tep!

We waited until the Bradhi had reached the ground and then, as the courtiers and guards surged forward, drew in our ladder, sliced our mooring lines and rose into the sky above the Jewelled City.

Now that I knew the truth—that I was really in the same time-period that I had been drawn away from earlier—I was determined to return to Varnal, City of the Green Mists, and see my Shizala. Also we had to discover what the Bradhi, Carnak—Shizala's and Darnad's father—knew of this business and what he was preparing to do.

The great battle which had taken place at Varnal between the Karnala and the Argzoon had badly depleted the Karnala force and wearied them. I did not think they could stand a chance of winning a war with the stronger Mishim Tep.

Neither, I thought, would their hearts be in it, for while those of Mishim Tep were convinced that Horguhl spoke truth, the Karnala knew otherwise and must feel more than sympathy for the delusions of their friends.

It would take us some time, even at full speed, to reach Varnal, but at least Darnad would be able to guide me.

As we sped towards the City of the Green Mists, Darnad told me what had befallen him since we had parted at the Caverns of Argzoon.

You will remember that Darnad and I had decided that one of us should return to the South to get help to rescue Shizala, who was Horguhl's prisoner in the Caves of Argzoon, if I was unsuccessful in my attempt.

He had left, riding as swiftly as he could over the hundreds of miles we had crossed. But his mount had gone lame shortly afterwards and he had found himself without a dahara in the heela-infested forests.

Somehow he had fought off those heela which had attacked him—though his beast had not been so lucky—but had lost his bearings a little and had stumbled on to a village of primitives who had captured him with the intention of eating him.

He managed to escape by burrowing out of the hut in which he was imprisoned but, weaponless and half starved, he had wandered for some time before meeting up with a band of nomadic herdsmen who had helped him.

Many more adventures followed and at length he was enslaved by brigands, who sold him to the representative of a Bradhi of a small nation that had somehow managed to survive in the South, though it was far behind most of the Southern nations in terms of civilization.

He had seized his first opportunity to escape from the working party and had headed for Mishim Tep, it being the nearest friendly nation—or so he thought.

Reaching Mishim Tep and telling the villagers of a small settlement near the border who he was, he was driven off as an enemy!

He could not believe what had happened and had decided that a mistake had been perpetrated.

He had found himself hunted by those he regarded as his nation's greatest allies. For weeks he had eluded the guards who sought him, but had eventually been cornered. He had fought well but had finally been captured.

The guards had taken him to Mih-Sa-Voh, where I had first seen him.

It was a story to match my own—which I told him at his request.

Soon we were flying over the vast plain which I recognized at once from the weird, crimson ferns which covered it, undulating slowly in the breeze like an endless ocean—the Crimson Plain.

I welcomed the sight for it meant we were fairly close to the Calling Hills in which lay Varnal, City of the Green Mist, home of the Bradhis of Karnala—and Shizala, my betrothed.

The Calling Hills were reached next morning and it was no time before we had reached the valley where lay Varnal.

My heart leapt in joy as I saw again the tall white buildings of Varnal. Here and there some of the buildings were of the strange blue marble which is mined in the hills. Traceries of gold veined the marble, causing the buildings to glitter in the sun. Pennants flew from the towers. It was a simpler city than Mih-Sa-Voh, the Jewelled City, and not so large, yet to me it was infinitely more beautiful—and an infinitely more welcome sight!

We dropped down into the city square and guards came forward at once, very alert, preparing to treat us as enemies.

The Bradhi Carnak hurried down the steps of his palace, Shizala following him.

Shizala!

She looked up and saw me. Our eyes met and locked. We stood there with tears of joy coming to our eyes, then I was leaping from the cabin and hurrying forward to take her in my arms.

"What happened?" she asked. "Oh, Michael Kane, what happened? I did not know what to think when you disappeared the night before the betrothal ceremony. I knew you would not leave me of your own volition. What happened?"

"I will tell you soon," I promised. "But first there are other things to discuss." I turned to the Bradhi. "Did you know that Mishim Tep plans to march against Varnal?"

He nodded grimly, sorrowfully. "The declaration arrived by herald yesterday," he said. "I cannot understand how Bolig Fas Ogdai came to believe these perversions of the truth. He accuses me and mine—and you, Michael Kane—of the most heinous deeds known to our society. We were friends for many years, our fathers and forefathers were friends. How could this be?"

"I will explain that, too," I said. "And now, let us try to forget these problems—we are united once more."

"Yes," he agreed, trying to smile, "this *is* a day of joy—to see you both return together is more than I dared hope for. Come, come—we shall have a meal and will talk and learn everything."

Hand in hand, Shizala and I followed her father and brother into the palace.

Soon the meal was prepared and I began to talk, telling them of my return to earth, my journey back to Mars and my adventures in the North. Darnad then told of his adventures and we discussed what had been happening in Varnal since we had left.

In spite of the black cloud of imminent war that was forever present, we could not disguise our joy at being reunited and the talk went on long into the night. The next day would bring two things—the ceremony of betrothal between Shizala and myself, necessary before a marriage could take place, and plans of war...

CHAPTER FOURTEEN

An Unwelcome Decision

"So Horguhl has deceived Bolig Fas Ogdai as she deceived his son," said Carnak next morning.

"She has him totally in her power," Darnad said.

We were eating breakfast together—a rare custom on Mars, but there was little time to waste.

"There must be some way of convincing the Bradhi that she is lying," Shizala said.

"You have not seen him," I told her. "We tried to convince him, but he was hardly aware of what we said—he was like a man in a dream. This war is her doing—not Bolig Fas Ogdai's."

"The question remains," said Darnad, "how can we avert this war? I have no wish to shed the blood of my friends—and no wish to see Varnal destroyed, for they would undoubtedly win."

"There is only one way I can think of." I spoke softly. "It is an unwelcome solution—but there seems nothing else for it. If all else fails, someone must kill her. With the death of Horguhl will come the death of her power over the Bradhi and his subjects."

"Kill a woman!" Darnad was shocked.

"I like the thought no more than do you," I said.

"You are right, Michael Kane." Carnak nodded. "It must be our only chance. But who would take on such a repugnant task?"

"Since I reached the decision, then the onus must be on me," I murmured.

"Let us discuss this later," said Bradhi Carnak hastily. "Now it is almost time for the betrothal ceremony in the throne room. You and Shizala must prepare yourselves."

I returned to my chamber and Shizala to hers. There I found arranged a variety of accoutrements and clothing. In a short while Darnad arrived to show me how I must wear all this.

There was a harness made of finely beaten links of gold and silver, studded with gems, and a sword that also shone with jewels, with a matching dagger.

There was a thick cloak of dark blue lined with rich scarlet. The cloak was decorated with delicate embroidery in yellow and green thread depicting, symbolically, scenes from the history of the Karnala.

There were also a pair of sandals of soft, shiny black leather that laced up to just below the knee.

Soon I was dressed in all this and Darnad stepped back admiring me.

"You make a fine sight," he said. "I am proud to have you as a brother."

There was no such term as "brother-in-law" in the Martian vocabulary. When one married into a family one automatically became of the same status as a blood relative. I would become Carnak's son and Darnad's brother—their brothers and cousins would become mine. It seemed strange that, by this logic, Shizala would not only become my wife but also my sister and my niece! But that was the custom of Mars and I would accept it.

Darnad led me to the throne room where a few chosen courtiers awaited us. The throne room was not unlike that at the Jewelled City, though simpler and less pretentious. On the dais stood the Bradhi Carnak in splendid robes of black fur, a circlet on his head.

Like most of the important customs of Southern Mars, the ceremony was short and yet impressive.

Carnak announced that we were to be married and we affirmed that it was our wish and the wish of no-one else that this should be. He then asked if there was any objection to this marriage. There was none.

Carnak concluded: "Then let it be that my daughter Shizala, the Bradhinaka, and my son, Michael Kane of Negalu, be wed when it should please them after the period of ten days from this."

And so I became engaged to that wonderful girl.

There was nothing for it but to prepare for the worst. On a balcony in a tower of the palace we looked down at the square beneath as our pitifully depleted army began to assemble.

I had divested myself of the ceremonial robes and was now clad in a simple warrior's harness, with a workman-like sword and one of the somewhat inaccurate, air-powered pistols of the Karnala. Over my shoulders was draped a cloak of dark green cloth.

I might remark, too, that I was beginning to let my hair grow longer, in the fashion of the Southern Martians. Though this custom is frowned on in our society to some extent, short hair on Mars is conspicuous and one is inclined to be questioned about it. Thus, to conduct myself as much as possible like my hosts—whom no-one could call unmanly!—I was allowing my hair to flow! It was kept from my eyes, also in the Southern Martian manner, by means of a simple metal circlet. Mine was of gold and had been a betrothal gift from Shizala. I stood now with my arm around her as we looked into the square.

As chief Pukan-Nara of Karnala's warriors, Darnad was in the square, but Carnak was with us on the balcony.

"Have you been able to judge the strength of Mishim Tep?" Carnak asked me.

"I have," I replied. "To some extent, at least. They must outnumber you five or six to one!"

"Our strongest ally turned against us! This will mean the destruction of the South as we know it," Shizala said wearily. "For centuries the balance of power has been held by what we choose to call the 'benevolent nations,' Mishim Tep and Karnala chief among them. This war will weaken us to such an extent that the South will become prey to all kinds of enemies."

"Doubtless that is exactly what Horguhl is hoping," I pointed out. "In the anarchy that must follow this war—and it cannot matter to her who wins it—she will gain the power she lusts for. She failed in her attempt to smash us by use of the Argzoon—now she tries this. She does not give up easily."

"She is a strange woman," Shizala said. "I spent much time in her company—forcibly, of course, since I was her prisoner. Sometimes she appears so innocent and bewildered, at other times she is a monster! And that weird power of hers—that ability to make others do what she chooses—it is inhuman."

"It is not inhuman," I said, "since many must have a similar power, though not so well developed. It is the use to which she puts it that is perverted!"

"She seems to blame all Southern nations for some crime committed against her," Shizala said. "Why is that?"

"Who can explain the motives of a sick mind?" I said. "She is insane—and if insanity were easily explained by logic, then perhaps there would be no insanity!"

"This plan of yours," said Shizala with a slight shudder. "The one to kill her. How do you plan to make the attempt?"

"It is so distasteful to me," I said, "that I have not thought much about it. First we must wait until the main army of Mishim Tep is on the march. I do not think that Horguhl will risk her own life by riding with the army. She will remain behind. I would only—only kill her, of course, in the last resort—that is, if I could find no other way of convincing the Bradhi that she lies. Or, better still, forcing her to admit that she has not told the truth!"

"And when the army is on the march—what then?"

"I will enter Mishim Tep in secret."

"How?"

"I will travel most of the distance by airship, then stain my skin roughly the same colour as the men of Mishim Tep, entering the city as a mercenary. I believe there are bands of mercenaries who seek employment in Mishim Tep."

"They are the Jelusa—cousins to the men of Mishim Tep."

"Then I shall become a Jelusa."

"And what then?"

"Ask to speak with Horguhl alone, telling her I have secrets…"

"She will recognize you!"

"Is it not a custom amongst the Jelusa mercenaries to mask themselves so that none shall know who has been hired?"

"It is."

"Then I shall be masked."

"And when—if your attempt succeeds—you are alone with her?"

"I will try to kidnap her and get her to write out the truth. Then I will imprison her and take the statement to the Bradhi of Mishim Tep. If he still refuses to accept the truth I will show it to his nobles. I am sure they will see it, not being directly under her spell..." My voice trailed off as I saw Shizala's expression.

"It is a daring plan," she said—"but it is almost bound to fail, my love."

"It is the only plan I have," I said, "the only one with the slimmest hope of succeeding."

She frowned. "I remember Telem Fas Ogdai once telling me of an almost forgotten object which they have at Mih-Sa-Voh, in their treasure house. It is a shield with a polished surface that transfixes anyone who gazes into it."

I was interested in the tale, since it seemed to have affinities with our own tale of Perseus and the Gorgon—and, perhaps, since our race is descended from that of Mars, that was the origin of our legend. "Go on," I told my betrothed.

"Well, this shield has another property. Anyone who looks into it is forced to speak the truth. It is something to do with the mesmeric effect of the surface. I do not know the scientific explanation, but it was probably designed by the Sheev or the Yaksha, and their science was far ahead of my knowledge."

"And mine, too," I said.

"I think it is only a legend—an amusing story Telem Fas Ogdai told to while away an hour."

"It sounds unlikely," I agreed—then dismissed the thought from my mind. I could not afford to waste time on speculation.

Shizala sighed.

"Are we never to know peace, Michael Kane?" she said. "Has some other power decided that a love so rich as ours may not be enjoyed in tranquility? Why must we continually be parted?"

"If I am successful, perhaps we shall have a chance to spend long years together in peace," I said comfortingly.

Again she sighed and looked into my eyes. "Do you think that is likely?"

"It is worth striving for," I said simply.

The next day we stood again on the balcony.

"The army of Mishim Tep must be on the move by now," she said, "and marching towards Karnala. It will take many days before they reach us."

"That gives me so much longer to do what I must," I said. I knew she was hinting that we could spend a few more days together, but I could not afford to risk anything going wrong—must give myself as much margin of time as possible.

"I suppose so," she said.

I kissed her then, holding her close.

Later, looking down again into square, I watched the tiny force that only recently had to fight off a far larger force of Argzoon blue giants, making their preparations.

It had been decided to meet the army of Mishim Tep on a battlefield rather than wait for it to lay siege to the city. If possible the city, and its women and children, would be preserved. The army of Mishim Tep were not barbarians and once they defeated the army of the Karnala they would not make any further reprisals for any supposed insults and treachery we of Varnal had subjected them to.

Seeing the army making ready, I decided to waste no more time and to leave that very night for the Jewelled City.

I bid farewell to Carnak and Darnad. I said goodbye to Shizala.

I also said a silent goodbye to that lovely city as the waning sun stained its marble red as blood.

And then, the brief period of peace over, I was heading back towards Mih-Sa-Voh.

CHAPTER FIFTEEN
Assassin's Mask

I STOOD AT the gates of the Jewelled City and answered the challenge of the guard.

"What do you want within? Know you not that Mishim Tep is in a state of war?"

"That is why I come, my friend. Can't you see that I am of the Jelusa?"

In my mask of thin, filigree silver covering my whole face, my blood-red cloak and my sword carried in a sheath—a strange custom on Mars—I looked a perfect mercenary of the Jelusa. Or so I thought. Now that the guard gave me a careful appraisal I was not so sure.

Then he seemed satisfied.

"You may enter," he said. After a moment's delay the gates swung back and I strode through jauntily, a pack slung over my back.

The guard came down from the wall and confronted me.

"You have no dahara," he said. "Why is that?"

"It went lame on the journey here."

He accepted this and pointed up the street through the evening gloom.

"You will find the rest in the House of the Blue Dagger," he said.

"The rest? The rest of whom?"

"Why, the rest of your companions, of course. Were you not with the party?"

I did not dare risk denying this, so I went in some trepidation up to the House of the Blue Dagger—a lodging house and tavern—and entered. Seated inside were several Jelusa mercenaries in masks of bronze, silver and gold, some of them modeled in the shapes of alien faces, some studded with tiny jewels.

Since they did not acknowledge me, I did not acknowledge them.

I asked the tavern keeper if there was a room available but he shrugged. "Your fellows have them all. Would you share a room with one?"

I shook my head. "No matter. I'll find another tavern. Can you recommend one?"

"You could try the House of the Hanging Argzoon in the next street."

I thanked him and left. It was very dark now and I had difficulty finding my way through the streets. Street lighting seemed non-existent, even in the most civilized Martian cities.

I lost my way and never did find the tavern with the somewhat bloodthirsty name. As I quested around for another tavern I began to sense that I was being followed.

I half turned my head, trying to see out of the corner of my eye if there was anyone behind me, but the mask obscured my view—and I did not want to risk removing it.

I continued to walk on and then took a narrow side street, little more than an alley, and flattened myself in a doorway.

Sure enough, a figure passed me somewhat hurriedly. I stepped from my hiding place, drawing my sword.

"Is it polite, friend," I said, "to follow a man about in this way?"

He turned with a gasp, his own hand reaching for his shield.

Moonlight flashed on something and I realized he was wearing a Jelusa mask.

"What's this?" I said, speaking as jauntily as possible. "Do you seek to rob a comrade?"

The voice that issued from the mask was cool now. The man did not bother to draw his sword.

"It is against the code of the Jelusa to do any such thing," he said.

"Then what do you want of me?"

"A peep behind the mask, *friend*."

"That, too, is against our code," I pointed out.

"I do not know what your code is, friend, but I know the code of the Jelusa well enough. Do you?"

Evidently I had made some mistake and this man had noticed it. Perhaps there was some secret sign that Jelusa exchanged without apparently seeming to acknowledge one another.

It appeared that I would have to kill this man if he threatened to reveal my secret. Too much was at stake to risk his giving me away and thus ruining my whole plan.

"Draw your sword," I told him grimly.

He laughed.

"Draw!"

"So I was right," he said. "You are masquerading as a Jelusa."

"Just so. Now draw your sword!"

"Why?"

"Because," I said, "I cannot let you betray my secret—I must try to silence you."

"Did I say I was going to tell anyone what I know?"

"You are a Jelusa. You know that I am not, that I only pretend to be."

Again he laughed. "But the Jelusa might be flattered that you should wish to be one of them. There is nothing in our code that says we must betray a man or kill him simply because he pretends to be one of us."

"Then why were you following me?"

"Curiosity. I thought you were a thief. Are you?"

"No."

"A pity. You see—as you might know—the Jelusa Guild of the Masked is not only a guild of mercenaries and assassins, but of thieves also. It had struck me, my friend, that you might be here on the same errand as myself."

"What is that?"

"To rob the treasure vaults of the palace. After all, there are so few guards that it is an ideal opportunity. They are supposed to be impossible to rob, you know."

"I am no thief."

"Then why do you lurk behind a Jelusa mask?"

"My own business."

"You are a spy for the Karnala."

Since I was not a spy, I shook my head.

"This is very mysterious," said the Jelusa in his mocking voice.

Something occurred to me then. "How do you plan to enter the palace?" I asked him.

"Ah, so you have the same objects as me, after all!"

"I told you, I am no thief—but I would enter the palace without the necessity of approaching the guards."

"What is it then? Assassination?"

I shuddered. There was no point in lying—as a very last possibility, I was prepared to kill Horguhl if it would stop the two great nations from destroying one another.

"So that is it," the Jelusa murmured.

"It is not what you think. I am not a paid killer."

"An idealist! By the moons, I beg your pardon—I must be on my way. An idealist!" The Jelusa gave a mocking bow and pretended to try to hurry past me.

"A realist," I said. "I am here to try to stop the war which is imminent."

"An idealist. Wars come and go—why try to stop them?"

"That is scarcely an objective judgment coming from one who makes his living from war," I said. "But I'm tired of this. Will you swear silence about me, or will you draw your sword?"

"In the circumstances, I will keep silent," said the masked man, his golden, jewelled mask suddenly flashing as a ray of moonlight caught it. "Though I have a suggestion. I promise I will pry no more into your object for entering the palace—and I think my proposal will be to our mutual advantage."

"What is it?"

"That we help each other to gain entrance to the palace, then we go our different ways—you to the—er—victim, me to the treasure house."

It was true that I could do with an ally, though whether this cynical thief was exactly the ally I would have chosen I did not know.

I thought over his suggestion.

Then I nodded.

"Very well," I said. "Since you are probably more experienced in these matters than I, I will do as you say. What is your plan?"

"Back to the House of the Blue Dagger," he said, "and the privacy of my room. Some wine, some rest—and some talk."

Somewhat reluctantly, I followed him back through the maze of streets, marveling at his sense of direction. Perhaps this thief would be more than useful, after all.

The thief did not remove his mask when we reached his room, though I removed mine. He cocked his head on one side. His mask was moulded to resemble a strange bird and gave him a grotesquely comical appearance.

"My Guild-name is Toxo," he said.

"My name—" I hesitated. "My name is Michael Kane."

"A very strange name. Yes, I have heard it, as you suspected."

"What do you think of the name?"

"I think it very strange, as I said. If you mean what have I heard and what do I think of that—well, what is the truth? I tell you, my friend, I believe nothing and everything. I am not a good Guild-member—others who had given you the sign and received no recognition would have been angrier than I."

"What is the sign?"

Casually, with his right thumb, he traced a small cross on his mask.

"I did not notice," I admitted.

"That sign is necessary when all wear masks," he said. "I should not have told you that, either. Many have tried to pose as Jelusa. It is the best disguise there is."

"Did anyone else notice?" I asked.

"I told them you had given me the sign but that you might need help finding a tavern. That was my excuse for following you."

"You are something of a renegade," I said.

"Nonsense—I simply live how I can. I do not believe in these stuffy guilds and the like."

"Then why don't you leave it?"

"The mask, my friend—the protection. I survive."

"Are there no penalties for speaking openly of the Guild's secrets?"

"We are more lax than we used to be, all of us—just a few fanatics keep up the old traditions. Besides, I cannot stop talking. I must talk all the time—so some of my talk must give away secrets. Still, what is a secret? What is the truth?"

This last seemed something of a rhetorical question so I did not bother to answer it.

"Now," said Toxo. "What about the palace?"

"I have only been in the main hall," I said. "I know little of its geography."

Toxo reached under the bed covering and produced a large roll of stiff paper. He smoothed it straight and showed it to me. It was a detailed plan of the palace, showing all windows and entrances, all floors and everything on them. It was an excellent map.

"This cost me my ceremonial mask," said Toxo. "Still, I never used it—and I can have another made when I am rich."

I was not sure of the morality of helping a thief rob a royal treasure house, but I thought the whole of Mishim Tep's jewels would be a small price to pay to avert the bloodshed that was about to happen.

"Why is there a guarded treasure house?" I asked. "Why, when jewels can be prised from the walls of the city and the inhabitants treat them like ordinary stones?"

"It is not so much the jewels themselves, which would fetch an excellent price some thousands of miles north or east of here, but the workmanship of the objects stored in the treasure-house," said Toxo.

He bent forward, his eyes gleaming at me from behind his ornate mask.

"Here is the best way into the palace," he said. "I rejected this means when I thought I was on my own."

"Would none of the other Jelusa help you?"

"Only one—and I know him of old for a bungling oaf. No, I am the only thief here at present—apart from the man I have men-

tioned. All the rest are simple fighting men. You should be able
to tell by the mask."

"I did not know there were differences in the masks."

"Of course!"

"Then what is mine?"

"The mask—as it happens—of an assassin," Toxo told me
brightly.

I felt a shudder run through me. I begged providence that
I would not be forced to kill a woman, no matter how evil she
was.

CHAPTER SIXTEEN
Woman of Evil

IT WAS VERY still in the streets of the Jewelled City and Toxo and I, both masked, hugged the shadows near the palace.

There was a distinct disadvantage to the masks in that they both caught far too much of the little light there was.

Toxo had unwound a loop of rope from his waist. It was thin rope but very strong, he assured me. He pointed silently up at the roof where a flagpole stood close to the edge. The reason two men were needed was because the rope had to be looped around the pole so that both ends dangled in the street.

One man had to hold the rope while the other climbed and secured it, allowing the second man to climb up.

The guard on the roof passed. There was only one doing a circuit, taking twenty minutes. In normal times there would be three guards.

Toxo flung the rope expertly upwards. It went snaking away to encircle the pole and one end flopped down on the other side, dangling over the edge of the roof. Now Toxo began to make little jerking movements on the rope and the short end, which had been weighted, began to slide down the wall.

Soon both ends were of equal length. I tied one round my waist and took the weight as Toxo began to climb. There were still more than ten minutes left before the guard was due to return—but it was slow climbing.

At last, after what seemed an age, Toxo reached the roof and tied the rope round the flagpole. I began to climb. I felt as if my arms were dropping off by the time I had reached the top.

Quickly we untied the rope and, ducking, ran towards the shadow of a small dome on the roof.

The guard came past. He had noticed nothing.

The roof, though flat, seemed rough and slippery. Reaching down to touch it, I realized that it was encrusted with polished gems!

Toxo was pointing mutely at the dome. This, too, entered into our plan. It was of glass—coloured glass on a soft metal frame. Noiselessly, we had to remove enough of the glass to let ourselves in.

We began carefully to prise the frame open and bent it back after first removing the glass.

Twice the guard passed. Twice he did not see us—his attention was on the street!

Finally, we had made a hole large enough for us to pass through. Toxo went first, dangled by his hands for a moment and then dropped downwards. I heard a soft sound as he landed. Then I squeezed through the hole, dangled and let myself fall.

We were on a catwalk high above a darkened room—perhaps a banqueting hall, for it was not the throne room where I had first confronted Horguhl.

Toxo began to run along the swaying catwalk and it was only then that I realized if I had missed the catwalk I would have fallen to my death!

Now we reached a door, bolted on our side. We slid back the bolts and went through the door into a small chamber off which led stone stairs.

Down the stairs we darted but then slowed our pace when we saw light filtering upwards. The dim, blue radiance of the Sheeva near-everlasting light-globes. Almost all the Southern Martians had these.

We peered downward into a large room—a servant's simply furnished room by the look of it. On a bed a fat man lay, sprawled in sleep. Beyond him was the door.

Our hearts were in our mouths as we crept past the sleeping servant and gradually eased the door open. We managed to do it without waking him.

Now we came, further down, to a larger room. This was better furnished and seemed to be the living room of a larger apartment—perhaps a noble retainer who lived in the palace. The man we had passed was probably his servant.

Just as we set foot on the floor of this room the door opened—and I saw the noble who had encountered me earlier in the throne room!

With an oath, he turned—probably to summon help—but I was across the room in an instant, my sword out, slamming the door and cutting off his exit!

"Who are you? Jelusa, eh? What are you doing here?"

He seemed a little shaken but not frightened—very few of the Southern Martians are cowards. He made to draw his sword but I placed my hand on his and nodded to Toxo.

While the noble was still puzzling out what was happening—he may have been brave, but he was far from clever—Toxo unhooked his scabbarded sword from his belt and raised it by the scabbard, striking the noble on the head with the hilt.

He dropped without a murmur, and we tied and gagged him.

To Toxo's surprise, I had insisted that there must be no bloodshed. The folk of Mishim Tep were misguided and had been influenced by an evil, clever woman, but they did not deserve to die for believing her lies.

Opening the noble's door we found ourselves on a landing. Several other doors led off it.

This was where Toxo and I had decided to part. Judging by his map—which he had bought from a dishonest servant of the palace—Horguhl's apartments were on this floor.

Toxo had no interest in Horguhl but every interest in the treasure vaults below.

Silently we parted, Toxo taking the stairs that led down from the landing, and I creeping further along the landing to the door I sought.

Cautiously, I turned the handle and the door did not resist. The room was in darkness.

Had I made a mistake?

I can usually sense if a room is occupied, even though I cannot see.

This room was not occupied. I crept to the door leading off the room and found that the adjoining room was empty also—as were all the rest in the apartment.

I decided to risk switching on the light.

Surely I had not been wrong? Looking about me, I was sure that this was Horguhl's apartment—and yet she was not in it though it was late at night.

Had she ridden with the army after all?

I was sure she would not have done. She was brave enough, I will credit her, but it did not seem to fit into what I guessed of her scheme. She would prefer to sit back and watch the two old friends fight one another to the death.

Then where was she?

In the palace, I was sure. Now I would be forced to seek her out.

I left the apartments and went out on to the landing. Evidently the palace was for the most part deserted. All the usual occupants had left with the army and only a few guards and servants remained—with the noble we had encountered probably left to supervise them.

I decided to risk a visit to the throne-room, since instinct told me it was a likely place for Horguhl to be.

With a wary step I made my way down the stairs for several flights, until I reached the ground floor, coming to the entrance hall I recognized.

I ducked hastily back into the shadows as I saw that a guard was on duty by the doors of the throne room. Only one dim, blue bulb burned above his head. He seemed half asleep.

Somehow I had to distract his attention so that I could enter the throne-room.

In my belt was a small knife I had used to prise away the soft metal of the dome on the roof. I took this out and threw it from me. It landed near the opposite staircase on the other side of the hall. The guard jerked himself into full wakefulness at the sound and peered towards the other staircase. Slowly he began to walk towards it.

This was my chance. Swiftly, I ran across to the doors of the throne-room, my feet almost silent on the smooth floor. I inched open the doors, which I had noted earlier opened inward, and closed them softly behind me once I was through.

I had done it.

And there—on the throne of Mishim Tep—sat the woman of evil, that wild, dark-haired girl who was so beautiful and yet so peculiarly twisted in her mind. As Shizala had said, partially an innocent, partially a woman of preternatural wisdom.

She hardly saw me. She was sprawled in the throne looking upwards and murmuring something to herself.

I had a little time to act before she called the guard. If she called, more than one were sure to come. I sprinted up the hall towards the throne.

Then her eyes dropped and she saw me. She could not have recognized me, for I still wore the silver mask. But, of course, she was startled. Yet her curiosity—a strong trait in her—stopped her from immediately calling for help.

"Who are you?" she said. "You in the strange mask."

I did not reply but began to walk towards her with a measured pace.

Her large, wise-innocent eyes widened.

"What do you hide behind the mask?" she said. "Are you so ugly?"

I continued to advance until I had reached the foot of the dais.

"Take off your mask or I will summon the guards, and they will remove it for you. How did you get in here?"

Slowly I raised my hand to my mask.

"Do you really wish me to remove it?" I said.

"Yes. Who are you?"

I snatched off the mask. She gasped. Several emotions flashed across her face and, strangely, not one of them was the hatred she had exhibited earlier.

"Your Nemesis, perhaps," I said.

"Michael Kane! Are you here alone?"

"More or less," I said. "I have come to kidnap you!"

"Why?"

"Why do you think?"

She literally did not seem to know. She put her head to one side and looked into my face, searching for some sign—I knew not what.

Regarding her, I found myself unable to believe that this girl-like person sitting on the throne could be capable of such hatred that it could bring down whole nations. Already she had been responsible for using the Argzoon to weaken the power of half-a-dozen Southern nations—and destroyed the Argzoon nation in the process. Now Karnala and Mishim Tep faced one another in warfare and she sat with innocent eyes quizzically staring into my face.

"Kidnap me...!" She seemed to find the idea almost attractive. "Interesting..."

"Come," I said brusquely.

Her eyes widened and I averted my own from looking at them directly. I knew her powers of hypnotism already.

"I would still know why, Michael Kane."

I hardly knew what to say. I had expected many things from her but not this near-passive mood. "To have you testify that you lied to the Bradhi about his son, about Shizala, about me—and so stop the war before it is too late."

"And what will you do for me if I do this for you?" She was almost purring now and her eyes had become hooded.

"What do you mean? Do you want to make some kind of bargain?"

"Perhaps."

"What bargain?"

"You should know, Michael Kane. You might almost say that it was because of you and for you that I created this situation."

I still did not understand.

"What do you propose?" I asked. It would be a relief if this was all she wanted.

"If I tell the Bradhi I lied, I want—*you*," she said, flinging her arms towards me.

I was shocked. I could not answer.

"I am leaving here soon," she said. "I need do no more than what I have done. You could come with me—there would be nothing you would want for if you did."

Playing for time, I said: "Where would we go?"

"To the west—there are lands in the west which are warm and dark and mysterious. Lands where strange secrets may be found—secrets that will bring us great power, you and I. We could rule the world!"

"Your ambition exceeds mine, I am afraid," I said. "Besides, I have had some experience of the Western continent and would not return there again willingly."

"You have *been* there!" Her eyes lighted and she stood up, stepping off the dais to stand close to me and look up into my face.

I was still at a loss for something to do or say. I had expected a screaming mass of hatred—but found her in this weird mood. She was too subtle, perhaps, for me.

"You have been in the west," she went on. "What did you see?"

"Things I would not wish to see again," I said. Now I was involuntarily looking into her eyes. They drew all my attention. I felt my heart beating strongly and she pressed her body against mine. I could not move. A voluptuous smile played about her lips and she began to stroke my arm. I felt dizzy, unreal, and I heard her voice coming to me as if from a distance.

"I swear," she was saying, "that I will adhere to my side of the bargain if you will adhere to yours. Be mine, Michael Kane. Your origins are as mysterious as the origins of the gods. Perhaps you are a god—a young god. Perhaps you can give *me* power, not I you."

I was sinking deeper and deeper into those eyes. There was nothing else. My flesh felt like water. I could hardly stand. She reached up and began to run her fingers through my hair.

I swayed and stumbled backwards and the movement helped me break her spell. With an oath, I pushed her away, shouting:

"*No!*"

Her face changed then, contorted with hatred.

"Very well—let it stand," she said. "I will enjoy putting you to death myself before I leave. Guards!"

A single guard entered.

I drew my sword, cursing myself for a fool. I had let Horguhl beguile me as she had beguiled the Bradhi. Her powers had even increased since the last time I had encountered her. If they increased any more, heaven only knew what would happen. She had to be stopped by some means—any means!

The guard swung his sword at me and I parried it easily. I do not boast when I say I am a master swordsman and easily the match for an ordinary palace guards. I could have finished him speedily but I was still wishing not to have to kill. I tried the trick of flicking his sword from his hand, but he held on to his blade too tightly.

While I was wasting time trying to disarm him, several more guards rushed in.

Horguhl was at my back as I defended myself now against six swords—and I still fought an entirely defensive action since I was anxious not to kill.

It was my undoing, for while I engaged the guards Horguhl had come up behind me with some heavy object—I never knew what it was—and struck me a glancing blow on the head.

I fell backwards.

My last memory was of cursing myself roundly again for the fool I was.

Now everything seemed lost!

CHAPTER SEVENTEEN
The Mirror

I AWOKE IN a dank cell that was plainly somewhere underground. It was not primarily a prison cell—the Bradhis of the
South are not like the old mediaeval robber barons of Earth—
but had probably been used for storage purposes. The door was
strong, however, and no matter how I tried to shift it I could not.
It was barred on the outside.

My weapons had been taken away from me.

I wondered what fate Horguhl planned for me. In refusing her
proposals of love I had redoubled her hatred for me. I shuddered. Knowing what sort of thoughts her mind could turn to, I
did not enjoy thinking of the prospect of torture at her hands.

There was a small chink in the door through which I could
see the bar. If I had had a knife I could have lifted the bar, I was
sure—but I had no knife.

I began to feel my way around the cell. There were bits of refuse here and there—crates of vegetables seemed to have been
stored in the cell.

My hand touched a wooden slat and then passed on—until I
realized what the slat might promise. I picked it up and took it
back to the door, but it was too thick to pass through the chink.

The wood was not hardwood but quite soft. This gave me an
idea. Carefully, with my thumbnail I began to try to split it sideways.

Little by little I worked at the slat until I succeeded. Then I
returned to the door and the tantalizing chink and—my piece of
wood went through.

Thanking my stars that the cell had not been designed with
the idea of imprisoning anything more than a few crates of vegetables, I began to inch the bar upwards, praying the thin slat
would not break.

After some time of this I finally managed to lift the bar.

It fell with a thud to the floor outside and I pushed the door open.

The corridor was in darkness. There was another door at the end of it. I walked up to this door, not expecting danger, and found myself confronted by a guard who was only just awakening from a doze. Evidently he had been disturbed by the noise of the bar falling.

He leapt up, but I flung myself at him. We began to wrestle across the littered floor, but then I got an armlock round his throat and squeezed the air from him until he passed out. Then I rose, took his sword and dagger, and continued on my way.

The corridors beyond the first one were a maze, but at length one widened out into a rather impressive corridor, high and roomy, leading towards a pair of heavy doors which seemed to be of solid bronze or some similar metal.

Perhaps these led to the stairs up to the main palace, I thought hopefully.

I opened the doors—and was confronted by one of the strangest sights of my life.

It was the treasure house of Mishim Tep, a huge vault with a low roof. In it were stacked works of the finest craftsmanship—indeed, artistry would be a better word. There were jewelled swords and chalices, chairs and great tables, pictures made of precious stones that seemed to give out their own light. All were dusty and piled at random. Careless of their treasures, the Bradhis of Mishim Tep had stored them in darkness and all-but forgotten about them!

I gasped at the wonder of it and could only stand there staring.

Then I saw Horguhl. She was absorbed with something, her back towards me. Even as I walked through the heaps of art treasures she did not seem to notice me. I took my dagger out and reversed it, planning to knock her on the head.

Then my foot slipped on a jewelled mosaic and I stumbled against one of the piles with a crash. It fell—and I fell with it.

From the corner of my eye I saw Horguhl turn and snatch up one of the swords.

I tried to rise, but my feet slipped again. She raised the sword and was about to bring it down into my heart when she suddenly stood transfixed.

Her mouth gaped open. She was not paralysed—not in the way I had been when injected with the poison of the spider-men—but her muscles became slack and the sword dropped from her nerveless fingers.

I turned my head, wondering what she had seen, but a shout sounded suddenly:

"Do not move!"

I recognized the voice. It was Toxo's. I obeyed his urgent order.

A little later the voice came again. "Stand up, Michael Kane, but do not look back."

I did as he said.

Horguhl still stood transfixed.

"Move to one side."

I did so.

A little later I saw the bird-mask and the bright little eyes gleaming behind it.

"I found the treasure vaults." Toxo patted a large sack he carried over his shoulder. "But this young woman disturbed me. Evidently she was engaged in a similar project."

"So this is what she planned," I said. "She told me that if I went with her we should want for nothing. She was not only scheming to bring catastrophe to Mishim Tep and Karnala, but to escape with the treasures as well. But what did you do to her?"

"I? Nothing. I was trying to come to your aid when I, too, slipped and grabbed at the nearest support. I seized some fabric—it must have been very old—and it ripped in my hand. I exposed some kind of mirror. I was just going to look and see what I had done when I noted the effect that mirror had on the young woman, so I thought it wise not to look after all. Then I shouted a warning to you."

"The mirror!" I gasped. "I have heard about it—an invention of the Sheev. Somehow it manipulates light so that whoever looks into it is mesmerized. More than that, it will destroy their will so that any question asked of them will bring forth the truth."

This was Toxo the opportunity to repeat his favourite rhetorical question: "Ah, but what is truth? Do you think the mirror can really do all that?"

"Let us try," I said. "Horguhl—did you lie to the Bradhi of Mishim Tep about Michael Kane, Shizala and the rest?"

The voice that answered was weak but the word was clear enough.

"Yes."

I was jubilant. A scheme was forming in my mind. Keeping our backs to the mirror and our faces towards Horguhl, Toxo and I bound the girl, gagged her and—as a precaution against her own hypnotic powers—blind-folded her. The moment her eyes were covered she began to struggle—but she was far too securely bound for her struggling to get her free!

For good measure I wrapped her in my cloak.

"We shall need your cloak too, Toxo," I said. We made a wide detour through the heaped gems until we were behind the mirror. Like all the treasures of Mishim Tep this, too, had been forgotten. How many centuries had this subtle invention lain gathering dust? Many, by the feel of the rotten fabric.

We draped Toxo's cloak over the mirror and wrapped it up. It was about a foot in diameter and was set with only a few gems. It was circular in shape and very heavy, with a handle like that of a shield. Perhaps it had been used as a weapon by the Sheev, but I thought not. Probably, if it had been used in war at all, it had been designed as a method for getting information from prisoners.

Somehow we managed to get both girl and mirror—and also Toxo's loot—out of the chamber and make our way to the roof without being seen.

The guard was still patrolling—or if it was not the same guard it was one very like him. We tapped him on the head—we had no time for caution—and left him dreaming on the roof as we used the rope to lower our bundles to the street.

Once in the street we sneaked along, pausing every so often to rest.

I was praying that, having so far succeeded, we should not now be caught. Everything depended on me reaching the airship. I told Toxo of this and he was interested.

"We shall need mounts to reach it," he said as we came to the House of the Blue Dagger—which was at sleep, thankfully. We took our prizes to our room and Toxo left. He was away for half an hour and when he returned his eyes were gleaming with pleasure.

From somewhere he had stolen a carriage—a fast one, by the look of it—to which was harnessed a team of six daharas.

Toxo bundled Horguhl and me, together with his loot, into the back, covered us with a blanket, drew a hood over his face and whipped up the daharas.

I remember only being jolted along at an almost incredible speed. I remember an angry shout—from the guard at the gate, Toxo told me later—and then we were bumping over open countryside.

It was morning when I poked my head out from under the blanket. Somehow, in spite of the jolting, I had fallen asleep. Toxo was nudging me.

"You must guide me now," he said.

I guided him willingly to where I had hidden the airship. We drew aside the brush and there she was, unharmed. We began to load everything into the cabin, Toxo telling me that he would like to be dropped on the borders of the Crimson Plain near the robber city of Narlet—a city I knew well, a place of thieves and brigades where Toxo doubtless felt at home.

I agreed, since this was on my way. I was hoping to reach the two armies before they became engaged in conflict.

We were soon in the air and I stopped only once to allow Toxo to disembark with his sack of treasure, waved my thanks to the masked thief and then was rising again.

A few groans from Horguhl did nothing but assure me that she still lived—which was all I wanted to know at that stage.

Would I be in time?

CHAPTER EIGHTEEN
The Truth at Last!

THERE THEY WERE! I could not have left it any later!

The two armies—the large one of Mishim Tep and the smaller one of Karnala—were camped opposite one another on the Crimson Plain. It was a strange place to fight a battle, but doubtless the army of Mishim Tep had not expected to meet the Karnala at all—and the Karnala had simply marched until they encountered the Mishim Tep.

I could see their battle lines drawn up ready for the charge.

I could even see Carnak seated on his great dahara, with Darnad beside him, at the head of his men.

And there was the Bradhi of Mishim Tep, stern-faced, less glassy-eyed from what I could see—evidently Horguhl's hypnotizing powers did not last indefinitely—at the head of his large army.

As my airship began to descend they all looked up—recognizing it at once. A few spears were flung at it from the ranks of Mishim Tep, but the Bradhi raised his hand to stop his men. He seemed curious.

I took my makeshift megaphone from its locker and shouted down to the Bradhi.

"Bradhi, I bring you proof that Horguhl lied—that you are about to engage in a senseless war entirely because of the lies of one evil woman!"

He passed a hand across his face. Then he frowned and shook his head as if to clear it.

"Will you allow me to descend and prove this to you?" I asked.

After a pause, he nodded wordlessly.

I lowered the ship until the cabin was bumping the tops of the crimson ferns. Then, unceremoniously, I threw out the bundle that was Horguhl and, clutching the covered mirror in my hands, leapt after her. Swiftly I moored the ship and then dragged both the bound, gagged and blindfolded girl and my mirror over until I was standing in front of the ranks of Mishim Tep.

First I uncovered Horguhl and was rewarded by a gasp and a murmur. The Bradhi cleared his throat as if to speak but then changed his mind. Grim-lipped, he nodded at me again.

I took off the girl's gag, forcing her to stand upright.

"Will you believe the truth from Horguhl's own lips, Bradhi?" I asked.

Again he cleared his throat.

"Y-yes," he said. Already his eyes were brightening visibly.

I pointed at the wrapped mirror. "I have here the legendary Mirror of Truth which the Sheev invented millennia ago. You have all heard of its magical properties. I shall demonstrate one of them now!"

With my back towards the men of Mishim Tep, I lifted the mirror-shield by its handle and pulled away the covering. Then I reached out and removed Horguhl's blindfold.

At once the mirror drew her eyes and she stood again slack-mouthed.

"You see?" I said. "It works."

They began to crowd closer to see that I spoke the truth. "Do not look directly into the mirror," I warned them, "or you will suffer the same effects. Are you ready to see if Horguhl told truth or lies to the Bradhi and seduced you all into launching this needless war against your age-old allies?"

"We are," said the Bradhi's voice from behind me, surprisingly deep and firm now.

"Horguhl," I said slowly and clearly, "did you lie to the Bradhi?"

The low, now spiritless, mindless voice said: "I did."

"How did you convince him?"

"By my powers—the powers in my eyes and my head."

A gasp and a murmur at this. Again I heard the Bradhi clear his throat.

"And what lies did you tell him?"

"That Michael Kane and Shizala planned to kill and disgrace his son."

"And who was really responsible for this?"

"I was!"

A roar went up then and the men began to move forward. I was sure many of them—none had really wished to fight this battle against their ancient allies—were ready to tear her to pieces. But the Bradhi stayed them.

Then the old man spoke. "It has been proved to me that I was prey to this woman's evil powers. At first I believed that my son was a traitor—but then, when she came to me with another story, I would rather believe that one. It was a lie. I believed her first lie. I believed all her other lies. Michael Kane was right—she is evil—she almost brought utter ruin to the South."

Then Carnak and Darnad cantered forward and Carnak and Bolog Fas Ogdai laid hands on each other's shoulders and spoke quietly to one another in terms of friendship. There were tears in the eyes of both men.

Horguhl was tied, gagged and bound again and placed in a supply wagon in which she would eventually be taken back to the Jewelled City, to be tried there for her crimes.

The Bolog Fas Ogdai and a few of his nobles returned with us in our airship to Varnal—and Shizala.

There is little more to tell you save that the Bradhi of Mishim Tep was an honoured guest at the wedding of Shizala and myself. We spent a blissful honeymoon as guests of the Bradhi and later returned to Varnal, where I began supervising the building of more airships.

In order to get supplies of helium gas we organized an expedition to Mendishar and the desert beyond. In Mendishar a rule of great happiness had begun, with Hool Haji on the throne.

What a welcome I received from him! He had become convinced I was dead.

When we arrived at the Yaksha city we found the fountain blocked and the last of the ghouls lying dead near it. They had not had the sense to clear it!

It was on our third expedition to Mendishar's desert—this time with a full fleet of airships!—that I decided to try a more complicated experiment, using the machines I had found in the forgotten city of the Yaksha.

You will remember that the work on my matter transmitter was connected with earlier work on laser rays. By investigating the construction of the Yaksha laser I was able to devise a method of building a matter transmitter that would send me back to Earth at almost the same instant I left.

That is how I am able to tell you my story.

Epilogue

"SO THAT IS the explanation!" I gasped, looking at Michael Kane. "You can travel at will now between Earth of our age and the Mars of yours!"

"Yes," he replied with a smile. "And, moreover, I have sophisticated the whole technique. There is not need to shift the transmitter around—it can be kept in your wine cellar!"

"In that case, I shall have to find a new place to keep the wine," I said.

"And what do you intend to do on Mars now?" I asked him.

"Well, I am a Bradhinak now, you know." He half smiled. "I am a Prince of the Karnala—a Prince of Mars. I have responsibilities. Karnala is still weak. Since it will take time to build up her manpower, I am concentrating on building up her new *air*-power!"

"And is the excitement all over—will there be no more adventures?"

Kane's lips quirked. "Oh, I am not so sure. I think there will be many more adventures—and I promise that if I survive them I will pay you more visits and tell you of them."

"And I will publish them," I said. "People will regard them as fantasies—but let them. You and I know the truth."

"Perhaps the others, too, will realize it some day," he said.

Very soon after that he left, but I could not forget almost his last words to me.

"There will be many more adventures!" he had said.

I looked forward to hearing them.

ABOUT THE AUTHOR

Michael Moorcock (1939-) has been recognized since the 1960s as one of the most important speculative fiction writers alive. Born in London, Moorcock began editing the magazine *Tarzan Adventures* at the age of 15, and quickly gained notoriety for his character Elric of Melniboné, an anti-hero written as a deliberate reversal of recurring themes he saw in the writings of authors like J. R. R. Tolkien and Robert E. Howard. Many of his works, including both the Elric books and those of his popular androgynous secret agent Jerry Cornelius, are tied together around the concept of the Eternal Champion, a warrior whose many incarnations battle to maintain the balance between Law and Chaos in the multiverse, a term popularized by Moorcock referring to many overlapping dimensions. In addition, Moorcock has also been recognized for his non-genre literary work, and his influence today extends into music, film, and popular culture. His writing has won numerous critical accolades, including the Nebula Award, the World Fantasy Award, the British Fantasy Award, and the Bram Stoker Lifetime Achievement award, and in 2002 he was inducted into the Science Fiction and Fantasy Hall of Fame.

PLANET STORIES™

Collect all of these exciting Planet Stories adventures!

THE ANUBIS MURDERS
BY GARY GYGAX
INTRODUCTION BY ERIK MONA

The father of Dungeons & Dragons follows Magister Setne Inhetep, wizard-priest and master sleuth, as he tracks a murderer from ancient Egypt to medieval England. But what if the gods themselves are behind the crimes?

ISBN: 978-1-60125-042-1

ELAK OF ATLANTIS
BY HENRY KUTTNER
INTRODUCTION BY JOE R. LANSDALE

A dashing swordsman with a mysterious past battles his way across ancient Atlantis in the stories that helped found the sword and sorcery genre. Also includes two rare tales featuring Prince Raynor of Imperial Gobi!

ISBN: 978-1-60125-046-9

CITY OF THE BEAST
BY MICHAEL MOORCOCK
INTRODUCTION BY KIM MOHAN

Moorcock's Eternal Champion returns as Michael Kane, an American physicist and expert duelist whose strange experiments catapult him through space and time to a Mars of the distant past—and into the arms of the gorgeous princess Shizala. But can he defeat the Blue Giants of the Argzoon in time to win her hand?

ISBN: 978-1-60125-044-5

ALMURIC
BY ROBERT E. HOWARD
INTRODUCTION BY JOE R. LANSDALE

From the creator of Conan, Almuric is a savage planet of crumbling stone ruins and debased, near-human inhabitants. Into this world comes Esau Cairn—Earthman, swordsman, murderer. Can one man overthrow the terrible devils that enslave Almuric?

ISBN: 978-1-60125-043-8

BLACK GOD'S KISS
BY C. L. MOORE
INTRODUCTION BY SUZY MCKEE CHARNAS

The first female sword and sorcery protagonist takes up her greatsword and challenges dark gods and monsters in the groundbreaking stories that made her famous and inspired a generation of female authors. Of particular interest to fans of Robert E. Howard and H.P. Lovecraft.

ISBN: 978-1-60125-045-2

NORTHWEST OF EARTH: THE COMPLETE NORTHWEST SMITH by C. L. Moore
INTRODUCTION BY C. J. CHERRYH

Ray gun blasting, Earth-born mercenary Northwest Smith dodges and weaves his way through the solar system, cutting shady deals with aliens and magicians alike, always one step ahead of the law.

ISBN: 978-1-60125-081-0

Pick your favorites or subscribe today at
paizo.com/planetstories!
